LET THE COLD HOUSE BREATHE

Alan De Silva

Edited by Stephanie Williamson

2009

TABLE OF CONTENTS

Thank you:

Kimberly Pearson, Russell Weigandt, Lisa H/P, Birdie Fussell, Kristen Malgeri, Dr. Rodda (Northern Arizona University), Mr. Lipman (Rutgers University), Roderick Lapid, Stacy Love, Sheena and James.

Thanks for inspiration: Perry Farrell, Maynard James Keenan, Fred Green (Tempe, Az), Sam Lersch, Trent Reznor, Chino Moreno, Al Jourgensen, Lydia Lunch, Christian V. Phillips, Albert Hofmann, Chris Kane, Jennifer Mazza, Darren Aronofski, Alex Grey, Chloe Sevigny, Zach De La Rocha, Ani Difranco, Henry Rollins, James Wolcott, Nunzilla, James O'keefe.

This book is intended to inspire those to look outside of themselves and their culture.

A NEW WATER

there may be a sign
or an awakening
for you

one you can see
from a
peak clear distance

and like a pure ocean wave
it will rush over your head
cleansing your thoughts
and purging your guilt

please father
drink this new water
it may make you
sick
this color
clear
but forever
new
you'll build yourself
again

☆ ☆ ☆

NEXT TELLER PLEASE

Camella finally told me about her problem.

She hadn't told anyone until that night at the pool hall. We were on our third game when she scratched off the 9, dropped her pool stick and began to cry. Veins of mascara ran down her cheeks as she tried shadowing her face with her long black hair.

"What's the matter?"

"I can't sleep anymore," she sobbed.

"You can't sleep? Did you try going to your doctor? Maybe there's some medication you can take."

"It's not like that. I mean, it's more like...*why...*"

She took a moment to compose herself, wiping the muddy tears from her face. She ordered a beer from the bar. After taking a tiny sip, she remained still; her eyes transfixed on the glass.

"It's that I have this problem or something where *I'm. . .*"

"It's ok." I said, rubbing her shoulder. She bit her lower lip. Her swollen, red eyes slowly rose to mine. Her child-like stare spoke the silent words: *Can I trust you?*

"I'm taking like 8 or 9 showers a night," she finally admitted. "I don't know why I'm doing it. I have no idea. Every time I try to sleep I feel this need, this need to feel warm and clean. Safe, you know. A part of me wants to wash everything away and just like . . . *feel again.*"

At first I wasn't sure how to respond. I had always known Camella as someone behind the shattered mirror. Usually it was her vague smile that threw me off, a smile that never seemed to match her depressed eyes. It was if there was someone behind the face contorting expressions away from a dark past. But I knew that through all her pain and psychological repressions she wouldn't give up. She'd keep trying, forcing her will to climb the mountain of solace—that steep climb, where once on top one could finally see the hidden rainbow of happiness.

"You're probably just going through a tough time right now," I said.

"I feel like I'm not normal or something. And I feel really bad about Greg."

Greg was her last boyfriend. Everything seemed fine. Then one night out of the Scarlet Red she randomly cheated on him. As far as I knew there were no problems, no prior separation or substantial arguments—just one drunken night she decided to be with another guy. She later regretted her decision. Said the guilt saturated her heart: "It felt like it built up; it built up so much. Eventually it was like it shot through my veins, like these eels or something weaving through my body. It was so much. I couldn't take it anymore. But every night it kept picking away at me, kept forcing me to think. I sat up late thinking why? Why did I do it? I felt like slicing my skin and letting it all bleed to the floor. It's crazy, I know—and I don't want to hurt anyone. I don't. I just wish I could bring it all out, you know? I wana start saying how I feel for now on. This is me, how I feel. I don't want to feel scared anymore."

Greg eventually sensed her guilt.

Another man veiled, speaking whispers through silent storms of murdered dreams. Greg knew something was wrong, he could feel it. So one night he found a way to force it out of her. Her admission sparked a violent break up. Shit was broken, bruises left on her arms. 2 years of good times were now finally over. Now there was another man, now she was left alone.

"I feel really bad about that whole thing," she said. "I wish it never happened."

"You should let it go. It was a mistake, but you have to move on."

"Should I text him?"

"Who, Greg?"

"Yes. I want to text him."

"Why would you do that?"

"I'm gonna text him," she said, pulling her phone from her purse.

I kissed her on the cheek and paid the tab. She said she was going to stay for a while, have a few more. She didn't want to go home and see all the same things, same blankets and curtains, same tv, same bed spread, the monotony of a boring existence caught within the four walls of her room.

The next day I went to the bank hung-over. I had applied for the teller position two months prior and did my best not to drink on work nights. Counting cash, sometimes 3,000 in ones, twisted the stomach. I had a love-hate relationship with the counting machine. It helped the process yet it filled the air with dust. On occasion the counting machine would malfunction, usually because of the dust built up on the cylinder. Giant clumps of hepatitis, leaving me weak and helpless to count every dollar by hand. The whole thing turned out to be dirty work dressed in collared shirts, fake smiles, and silk ties.

✵ ✵ ✵

Maria was the Head Teller, my direct boss. She was single, second-generation Italian, and fretful her birthday next month. The stigma of 30. The biological clock ticking. The traditional Italian family holding pressure to get married, have kids. What are you waiting for? Where's your boyfriend? *Shhh, I think there might be something wrong with her.* Out of pity every Italian customer did their best to set her up with their one degenerate son, nephew, or cousin. Maria was saddened by the experience, over emotional about it. She gradually began to despise men. I was the only man working at the place. The rest of the co-workers were women, and they were all married.

"You forgot to fill out a CTR form yesterday," she curtly remarked.

"I did?"

"You need to fill that out. Don't forget next time."

I went into the vault to get my cashbox. A part of me wanted to lock myself in, turn out the lights and sleep. Air-tight darkness, completely safe to dream away the nightmare of a working life. When I came out, I noticed Maria whispering to the Assistant Manager, Mary. I placed my box in the drawer and turned on the computer. The phone rang. "Thank you for calling the Leverage Bank. This is Jamison."

"Hi."

"Hello?"

"This is Debbie."

"Oh, hey."

"Is Maria around?"

"It looks like she's busy talking to Mary."

"Well, I called before. I'm running a little late for work but was wondering if anyone wanted something from Dunkin Donuts?"

"But you're late?"

There was long silence.

"What?"

"I said, but you're late."

"That doesn't have anything to do with you. You're just a teller."

"I know but it doesn't make sense. If you're running late then why would you take the extra time to get donuts?"

"Because that's just how we do things. Look, mind your own. Tell them that if they want anything they can call me on my cell."

I unlocked the cover to the box and logged on. 5 emails. Alert. Fraudulent checks. Identity theft. Mrs. Parker's drugged-out son stole her checkbook. Downloaded photos of snakes slithering across slimy river rocks. I sat in my seat and waited for a customer. Then Maria walked over and tapped me on the shoulder.

"How much money do you have?" she asked.

"I'm down to my last 30 cents, but I just paid rent."

"No, wiseass. I mean in your drawer."

"Just over 10, I think."

"I'm gonna count your drawer. Put your sign out."

Next Teller Please.

There was something about the sign that made me feel free. It was simple, black and white, carefully carved like eternal words on a dead man's gravestone. Last statement to the world, it moved people, grounded them to their fragile places. I felt this divine existence behind it, like I was an exception to the rule. Next teller. Next window. Move on, go somewhere else. And the fact that it said "please" compelled me to the notion that I was innocent in my feeble attempts to preclude myself from the world.

Maria began counting the hundreds, plugging the numbers in the computer as she went to lower denominations. She had a systematic way of counting money. It was fast, almost aggressive. She flipped through a stack of money, burning fibers, one hand to the next—her face focused, completely still. After counting the pennies, she entered the amount bringing my overall total to EVEN.

"You see?" I said. "And you still don't trust me."

"I have to audit you once a month. Make sure you don't pull a fast one on me."

I opened my station just in time for Mr. Daylo. An old man with a snail mouth and a pale face that sagged around the eyes. He called in 2,000 in tens. Had to be the new ones, no straps. House money for his wife. Said he'd be in around 11. At 10:20 he arrived. He only dealt with certain tellers. Unfortunately, I was one of them.

"How are you Mr. Daylo?"

"Splendid."

"Nice outside?"

"I suppose for this time of year."

I gave Daylo his money already pre-counted, pre-examined for wrinkles, marks, and tears. Daylo inspected regardless. A good 10 minutes at my window. About three quarters of the way he found a ten. He lifted the bill to the light. The translucency was off. Maria walked over with a few more tens. He went through them, methodically rubbing each one for the right texture.

"You know Alexander loves a good shoulder rub every now and again," he said, licking the crust from his perverted lips.

"Of course."

"Actually there are many historical references citing that his vision for the U.S. Treasury happened under the influence of his mistress's famous back rub."

"Really? I never heard that before."

He slowly looked up from his dirty nails.

"You have a good day now," he said, putting the money into an envelope.

"You too, Mr. Daylo."

Text Message … Camella Geller … 3:35pm.
Meet me at Plushmoo 6:30. He's not texting me back ☹.

For some reason I felt obligated to cater to her loneliness. Her madness. I had to go. And surely I would be swallowed again by an inspiring hole of gossip. Have a plan and work the plan, I thought. Keep it simple, have a few beers, and leave.

I arrived at the bar. At first I didn't notice her. Her once long and beautiful hair was now cropped and gelled tight to her head. With too much powder on her face, she looked like an alien out of an old Star Trek episode. She was sitting a few seats away from two girls. One of the girls, the blonde, I recognized from somewhere. I took the seat between Camella and the blonde. As much as I disliked Camella's new haircut, I had to say something to keep her spirits up.

"Like the hair. Where'd you get it done?"

"Axis."

"Nice. Did you just get here?"

"I took off early, got here at 4:30."

"4:30? How many drinks did you have?"

"I wana listen to Dave Mathews. Do you wana listen to Dave? I'm gonna put some Dave on the jukebox."

She walked over to the touch-screen jukebox. I ordered a drink. I looked at the blonde. Her tan face semi-ruined by the sun, piercing blue eyes that spoke of childhood happiness on a childhood farm. She had the look of experience. Why waste time. If you like me, approach me. I'm here. Be honest and don't play games. I caught her eye with a subtle smile.

"I've seen you before," she said.

"You have?"

"Yeah, somewhere. Hey, wait. Were you on the recent cover of *MG?*"

"I'm sorry?"

"Yes, with that cute little blonde girl staring up at the sky."

"I think you got the wrong guy."

"And the crystal ball. I saw you! You were wearing that same hat!"

Suddenly I heard Camella's voice: "Come on! What's the matter with this stupid thing?" I looked behind me and saw Camella frantically pushing the juke-box screen. I excused myself from the blonde and walked over. I approached the jukebox and noticed the screen was smeared with murky hand prints. Camella continued, slapping her hands against the screen, pushing with her palms, lifting the front end, slamming it back against the wall. Then in a fury, she closed her right hand and punched the glass.

"Hey, wait! You're going to break it!"

"NOTHING EVER WORKS OUT ANYMORE! THIS WHOLE FUCKING THING! I JUST WANTED TO HEAR DAVE! OH, PLEASE, DAVE! JUST THIS ONCE! OH, GOD! NO!"

Every ounce of her body and soul had violently ripped open. A waterfall of tears came as her legs suddenly gave out. She fell to the floor gasping for air. I knelt down and put my arm around her. "Hey, it's ok," I whispered compassionately. "It's temporarily out of order, that's all."

"All I wanted all day was to hear Dave. He makes me feel better. He just does, you know? I don't know what it is, but he's real ... and when I listen to him ... I don't worry about all the bullshit in this fucking world!"

"I know. I know. Hey, it's alright. I'll talk to the bartender, maybe he can fix it."

"I'm gonna go," she sternly said.

"Just one second. I'll ask him."

Out of the corner of my eye I saw her run out. I stood motionless, the blonde and bartender staring at me. I slowly made my way to the bar.

"Sorry about that," I said.

"It happens," the bartender said.

"So how do you know her?" the blonde asked.

"I met her at film festival. She's actually a pretty good actress."

"Looks like it."

I finished my beer and decided to leave. The blonde quickly approached me from behind. "Hey, wait," she said. I turned and looked. She stood silent for a few seconds. "You never asked me for my number."

"I'm sorry, I didn't realize. I guess I should."

"Well, you don't have to."

"No, I do. What is it?"

She peered deep, a sudden contrariety in her eyes.

"You know what, never mind."

She went back to her seat and began talking to her friend. I left out the front door, lit up a cig. A trail of smoke curled up to the sign: *Plushmoo Bar and Grill.* Two black birds building a nest on top of the letter *M*. One of the birds flew away. Then I remembered why I came. Camella. She wants to be free. That's it. Trapped. Now she's letting it go. I walked home wondering if she would be alright.

REHAB FOR A LOST IDENTITY

Rehab for a Lost Identity

"Anywhere you see the word *being* you can pretty much cancel that out."

—Chris Kane
GMAT Instructor, NYC, Fall 2007.

"I need my teeth pulled."
"I'm sorry, sir?"
"I need my teeth pulled ... *please. I...*"
"Sir? I can't hear you."
"My gums, fucking please."
Open mouth—
Thick pool of blood spills silent to the floor.
It's shortly after the clean up now, shortly after some time ago.
Light snaps and I see the moments pass. I try to make it out, colors—pictures. I know these beautiful pictures. I know them as they fade. Red and yellows always go on, they go on whether you can see them or not.

I lie sedated, the restraints around me, tight, holding me down. The sirens fell asleep but the red lights still flash passing cars. And the greasy hair meds are beside me doing their best not to look down.

The wheels quickly retract to the ground. I hear a squeak. It's persistent. The front wheel honing Entrance through a soft rain. Soon the sliding glass doors open to the sound of whispering waves. Circulating warm air shifting down, mixing the cool; this hot pressure against the Entered. The meds pushing, sweating through dark blue shirts. It's that sound, the squeak; it makes it worse. Itches. Deep. By the root. By the nerve of a lost soul.

This place bright and looming, through the main entry past a waiting room, a place stale, white lights, people trapped under a network of scattered consciousness. Intercoms, speakers between each fluorescent light, one after another; the ceiling moving like a conveyer belt, and seemingly slower than my ground speed. Here now. I can't really escape. The gurney keeps moving. And there are mirrors, maybe pictures, and silver, nurses in white. The sound of an elevator chime rings as we take a sharp left. I can already foresee him, dimpled-chinned, smelling of rubber, hands hairier than normal. Those knuckles are hard and dry, coming down, peeling skin as they bend. A dimmer light covered in plastic descends from the ceiling.

"Open your mouth for me please."

A shimmering rod, plastic tube.

My lips are not there. No face, just these eyes. Everything behind me is gone, hollowed by soft air. But the metal rod forces down, purging my mouth. It digs in with reflection. I can only see it for a second. Then a blur and the sound of a vacuum.

"60 milligrams of thorazine."

Everyone has left now. Only a room filled with light. Clorox-smeared chrome counter tops—and this bed and walls closing in. There is no texture, no patterns or color—everything sterile, abrasively normal. My limbs cannot move, just my eyes. I cannot fall asleep. I wish to sleep, only to sleep.

I went forth closing and opening my eyes. The dim orange blackness, intense white light, switching back—2 minute intervals in synch with the IV. These different shades of mind, contrasting murky shadows and open fields of clear.

2 minutes. I open my eyes. Here before me stands a nurse. She hovers with a calming smile. She is someone else; she is innocent, void of guilt, pure, radiant with the light.

"Do you know why you're here?" she asks in a soft voice. "You're here because you've left your past. You're here now—with us, safe. You've shed your skin and can now purge yourself vulnerable. The time has come for you to truly feel."

I blink my eyes and she is gone.

Then a tiny black dot from the ceiling begins to move. An insect or spider crawling patient to harm. It centers above me, then slowly lowers down, bouncing on splintered webs across a vast ceiling. It's coming towards my naval. It senses something. It waits. Just above. Then a single leg unfolds from its body. The retracting leg is longer than the rest. There are moments of pause, each conjoined segment needing time to unfurl. The final segment is needle-like. It comes out slowly. I suck in my stomach. I can only hold it for so long. I need oxygen. Let it breathe, this cold house. A desperate intake forces the stomach up and my naval is pierced by the long sharp leg.

☆ ☆ ☆

After four days in the hospital I found myself in rehab. An old church now defunct from the 50's prayer. The second floor torn out, exposing windows framed in by dusty beams. The sunlight penetrated through, °casting a bar code of light and shadow over a circle of chairs. And here, a sense the ocean near, with the sound of waves and seagulls faintly heard.

I sat with the rest of them. We waited in silence, each of us afraid to talk; the guilt of our presence oscillating through the air. Then an old wooden door cracked open. The councilor approached with the sound of forgiving footsteps.

"Hello everyone. For those of you who are new, my name is Professor Warren Lucus. I'll be your councilor for the next 9 weeks. Today, we're going to talk about how we deal with certain problems. As in, what is it that we do to control ourselves when we get angry or upset or even pressured into doing something we might not want to do. So I want you to think about a recent experience, and see what it is you did when dealing with it. Rick, since you've been here for a while, why don't we start with you. Take your time. Don't feel you have to start right away."

"You mean don't feel pressured?"

"That's right. Go ahead, start when you're ready."

"Well, I guess the most recent problem I had was loosing a bet on the Raiders."

"A bet?"

"Yeah, a bet."

"You bet on the Raiders?"

"I lost four-hundred dollars, man! My wife got mad after I threw my beer against the wall! It was a problem!"

"I see. Let's not forget why we are all here, ok. We need to try and stay focused on our overall goal of maintaining our sobriety. Let's not forget that. So if we're drinking or doing drugs then our judgment to make decisions is impaired. Remember what we said about drugs and alcohol and our judgment? What's the first thing drugs do?"

"Impairs your judgment," the group simultaneously announced.

"Good. Now, what's the second thing?"

There was a short silence.

"Who cares?" Lucus continued. "Remember? Who cares what the second thing is when our judgment to make decisions is impaired in the first place ... right? Ok, Joe, why don't we move to you next. So how have you been?"

"Good, I guess."

"Do you have anything you want to share with us?"

Joe. His eyes spoke of great pain, of bitterness against the world. He focused on the floor, eyes squinting to the agony. Uncontrolled thoughts. He desperately wanted the right words, to capture them in flight. He took a deep breath.

"I guess what bothers me the most is all these expectations. These expectations, they come like an unspoken rule for how you're supposed to live, or act, or even feel. I'm constantly fighting against it, like this tug of war with myself and the world. I wonder where it all fits sometimes. It confuses me, and sometimes it makes me feel like there's never a new day, like it's all one big lasting question ... I feel so different all the time, especially at my work. I'm constantly trying to find how to react and how to deal with it all. But that just causes me to trip, you know. Now they all see right through me; they look the other way, ignoring me like I'm an embarrassment. It's gotten so bad that no matter what I do, I mess it up. I'm sick of it, like I'm sick of the sun. I just am. Can't it rain for once?"

"That makes perfect sense," Lucus said. "It really does, Joe. We are all there with you, some of us feeling the same way. You're not the only one with this problem. Millions of people are dealing with the same thing, problems they can barely manage by themselves. We struggle through it, searching for the answers to our questions, and when things get tough we try to stick it out."

"Stick it out for what, though?"

"Stick it out for the experience of life. You have life, this playground to enjoy the feeling of being *alive*. It doesn't make sense to anyone; we're just here breathing, interacting with one another. There's no cure-all, no golden answer to everything. You just do your best to help yourself and others too. Progress, find your place. Does everyone agree? Ok, thank you Joe. I'm going to move onto Brad. For those of you who don't know, Brad is an artist. You can see some of his paintings at the Marion Gallery on Ocean Avenue. So, Brad, how are things going with you? Last time you spoke about the struggles in your relationship. How it may have drove you to your depression. Do you care to expand with us today?"

"Sure. We recently broke up … and as much as I am hurt from it, I think, ultimately, it was a good thing."

"Is there anything that you learned from the experience that you think might be helpful for the group? And, again, don't feel like you have to talk if you don't want to."

"No, it's ok. It would probably be good if I talked about it."

"Ok, go ahead and start when you're ready."

"After a while it got pretty bad. I was slowly beginning to realize that things weren't right with me—or at least I thought. I was made to believe that I was trapped in some type of fantasy world, and pretending to be some great person. I kept wondering why nobody could see it, especially her, why she kept turning her back on me. It was like everyone around me never looked deep, like they lived within the four walls that surrounded them. And that was it—that was their boundary. And the whole time this great emotion kept pouring in, over and over, floods of it drowning my bones and lifting me beyond the scope of reason. My girlfriend always used to say that I didn't give enough, that I was trapped in my own little world. I was supposed to treat her like a princess and give her all the love in the world, so much love that the whole world could explode and it wouldn't matter … because we would always be together. But it was happening all the same: these promises of opening up and letting go of the past. In a way I didn't want it to happen. I wanted to hold onto everything, good or bad, because without it, I too would be stuck behind the four walls. I would be stuck like them in this sorta void state with no drive for anything creative. I thought about giving it all up for her and this drove me to my depression. I was second guessing myself."

"That is a very perceptive point, and I want everyone in the group to take in what Brad just said. I'm honestly amazed. Does everyone see what's going on here? It's important to realize that being yourself is ok. That perhaps it might not always coincide with everyone else's views or beliefs, and sometimes it could be someone as close as a girlfriend or your mom or dad. If you try to deny yourself and blend in, then you're setting yourself up for disaster, as in this case with Brad. Now, of course, there are characteristics in everyone that are not good, and these are the things we need to work on changing, but there is a fine line between accepting yourself and finding the necessary grounds to change certain things that may be counterproductive. To recognize and act on the differences is what allows people to evolve. Very good, Brad. Now I want to move to Samantha. Samantha, how are you?"

"Good, I suppose," she said in soft, innocent tone.

"Do you have anything you want to share with us?"

"I'm not sure I have anything to say."

"Surely, there must be something you want to talk about."

"I don't know."

"Ok, no pressure. Why don't you just tell us what you want to do—something perhaps you look forward to in the future."

"What I want to do? You really wana know that?"

"Certainly. It doesn't always have to be about your past. Feel free to speak about anything."

"Well, I've been thinking lately—about leaving, going to Europe. I want to go to Amsterdam where they have all those tulips growing out in those big fields. You know the fields I'm talking about? And I wana go there and rent one of those bikes, not a regular bike like a mountain bike or something, but one of those bikes with the big handle bars. You know what bikes I'm talking about?"

"I think so. Like an old Schwinn?"

Samantha stretched her arms out, her hands reaching for the invisible handle bars.

"With those big handle bars. And I wana rent one and ride along and see all the beautiful tulips, fields of them looking so pretty. And just lay, lay with them and admire the sky, watching the clouds and feeling the air, so bright and so beautiful the *sky*..."

"That's a wonderful idea, Samantha. It's good that you're in touch with a lot of your feelings. You want to live your dream. And it doesn't matter what the dream is; it could be anything positive, something that helps you relax or perhaps something that inspires you. That's great."

I was next. I wasn't sure what to say. I thought about my experience, how I lost control. The hospital, the blood; how the nurse left me stripped, reborn. I thought about it, how those denied pains continued to ravage me without knowing why.

I sat there thinking. How does it all fit?

I began to speak. The words coming from somewhere deep within, about how our need for rehab was manifested under the delusion for escape; that truly we cannot escape, because we are One in a place where everyone's story is connected. Their stories were my stories, my stories were theirs, that we are never alone, even though the drug may have made it seem that we finally broke away from reality.

I finished my story and looked at the faces, confused faces. They held silent. I felt naked and fearful, wanting to escape again. Maybe I was wrong. Someone coughed breaking the silence. A bird flew across the room and the meeting was dismissed.

I left out the front door and waited for Samantha. I didn't know her, but I wanted to talk to her. For some reason, I had immediate feelings for her. I had this instant regard for her safety; I wanted to somehow guide her, to please her, to impart on a search for a common destiny—that peaceful existence out there in the field of tulips. She came out. Her glossy brown eyes glanced at me. I wanted to say something. She turned and walked away. I took a few steps towards her. My mouth opened, but no words. I just stood there and watched her body form smaller as she walked towards the ocean.

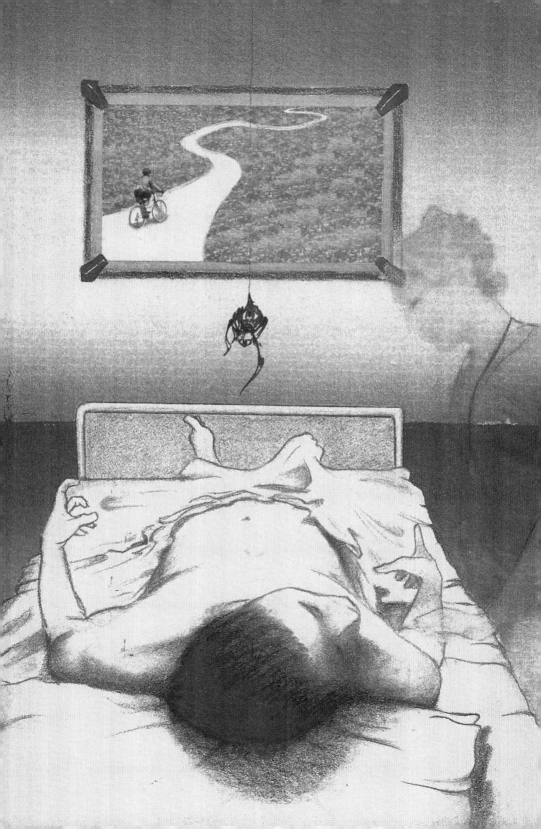

YELLOW OIL DRIPPING SATURN

Yellow Oil Dripping Saturn

Princeton Professor of Mathematics Omar Fourier sat at his desk and fathomed the possibility.

Then it happened. Omar gradually began to lose focus. Soon the equations blurred and a spec of haloed light appeared. The light danced across the page, flickering like a spark across a gray sky. How can an irrational number be stabilized? Uncertain and frustrated, Omar sharpened his pencil on the top right corner. He systematically rounded each edge, precisely turning the pencil a quarter at a time. Then in one fluid motion, he eloquently drew a series of spirals—each one sketched proportionately over the equations below. "It will be here soon," he whispered. "I just need a little more time."

Omar's six-year-old daughter Sylvia often complained of feeling cold. There had been many occasions when Omar noticed her in the hallway, dressed in two or three sweaters, an old ski cap covering her long blonde hair. She'd stand with her arms crossed, dissenting the discomfort. *"I'm cold,"* she'd whimper with crystal-blue eyes accentuating the feeling. It had been three years since Sylvia's mother died. Since then there had been gradual and subtle changes in Sylvia. Now there was something new, something deep within—born beneath her frail innocence.

Omar finished his work for the night and decided to check on Sylvia. Tucked beneath a heavy quilt that her grandmother made, Sylvia remained awake. She continued staring at the ceiling as her father entered the room.

"Dad?"

"Yeah, sweetie?"

"How many stars are in the sky?"

"Well, some people think there are an infinite number of stars."

Sylvia turned and looked at Omar.

"How many is infinite?"

"Well, infinite means it continues on, forever and ever."

"You mean it never ends, ever?"

"That's right—"

"But I see them. They're in the sky."

"Of course you do, and they're beautiful, right?"

"I'll count them tomorrow and see how many."

Omar became teary-eyed by his daughter's passion for the stars.

"Ok, sweetie. That's why I got you that telescope, so you can see them—and count them if you want."

"Ok."

Omar kissed Sylvia on the forehead.

"Do you want me to leave the door open tonight?" he asked.

"No, I'm fine."

Omar walked into the hallway, closing the door behind him. He stood for a moment and noticed the disparity in temperature. *Gosh, maybe she's right. It is kinda cold in here.* He walked down the hall, towards his bedroom door when suddenly he heard a noise from behind. He turned and noticed Sylvia standing with her arms behind her back.

"Sylvia?"

"I almost forgot."

"Forgot what?"

"I got you a present."

"A present? Present for what?"

"For Father's Day."

"But that was over two months ago." Omar quickly realized his parental mishap. He certainly didn't want to discourage Sylvia from being a giving person, so he continued gracefully, "Oh, well that's *so* nice of you. I'm honored. What is it?"

Sylvia slowly eased her arm out and exposed an envelope. Lining the square edges was a thin gold strip. On the front in big yellow letters, circled by orange hearts it read: *To My Dad.*

"Oh, wow!" Omar said. "Look at this! Thank you so much."

"You're welcome."

"Should I open it now?"

"No, you don't have to."

"Well ... ok. I guess it can wait till later if you want."

"Dad?"

"Yeah, precious?"

"You have to promise me something."

"Yeah, sure what is it?"

"You have to promise you'll go."

"Go where?"

"You'll see. It's in your present."

"Ok ... well, sure, I guess so. It's not something scary is it?" he said, poking at her stomach.

"No, dad," she sternly replied.

"Alright, alright, I promise."

Omar gently grabbed Sylvia under the shoulders and lifted her off to bed. After tucking her in, he returned to his room. He looked at his desk. A calm ambience, papers stacked high under a single light. The desk loomed in halogen glow, almost as if it were suspended away from the rest of the furniture. Omar sat down and put his glasses on—the envelope coming clearer. Where did Sylvia get this, he thought? Perhaps Aunt Lynda helped her? From the time Sylvia's mother died, Lynda had always tried to play surrogate mother.

Omar picked up the phone and dialed. A groggy, raspy voice answered. *"Hello?"*

"Sorry, Lynda. I hope I didn't wake you. I just wanted to thank you again for helping Sylvia find a gift for me."

"What?—Are you talking about your birthday gift?"

"No, not that. The envelope."

"I'm sorry?"

"You didn't help her find some type of card or gift certificate?"

"Gift certificate? What exactly are you talking about?"

"I'm not sure. I haven't opened it yet."

"Omar?"

"Yeah?"

"Why don't you open it?"

Omar analyzed the envelope. There was something strange about it. It was as if he had seen it before. He turned it over. At center, just above the seal, was a small crystal ball showing a fountain of stars shooting out the glass. He hesitantly tore at the corner when suddenly he heard a loud scream from Sylvia's room. He quickly hung up the phone and ran to Sylvia's side. Omar found her shivering, sitting upright in bed; her face white with fear, covered in sweat; and while trapped in point-blank stare, a nefarious voice involuntarily murmured, *"Ran...sire ... mun do potiri!"*

"Wake up sweetie!" Omar pleaded, shaking Sylvia's shoulders. "You're dreaming. It's ok." Then like a dim light building brighter, Sylvia's eyes came into focus. She looked at Omar, quickly wrapping her arms around him.

"What happened?" she asked.

"You were just having a bad dream. It's ok now."

Omar softly ran his hand through Sylvia's hair. Soon her breathing slowed and her shoulders eased from a tight tension. She cautiously rested her head back on the pillow as though frightened to fall back asleep.

"I'm going to leave the door open for you tonight," Omar assured her. "It'll help keep the bad dreams away."

"Dad?"

"Yeah, precious?"

"I counted them."

"You did? The stars? Well, that was quick. How many did you find?"

"1,635."

"That's a lot. Wow, I'm impressed. How did you count all those stars?"

Sylvia shrugged her shoulders and smiled. Omar instantly found comfort by the fact that her mind had drifted off to the stars and away from the bad dream. He leaned over and gave her a hug goodnight.

Omar entered his room. Immediately he noticed the envelope, the gold lining resplendent under the desk light. He hurriedly approached the desk and franticly ripped the envelope open. Inside was an invitation, a gypsy looking figure staring back with penetrating eyes, holding a crystal ball with the words just below, *Bright Shimmering Light and Welcome. One free psychic reading.* Omar was relieved only for a second before startled by the sharp ring of the phone.

"Hello?"

"It's me, Lynda. Is everything alright? The phone just hung up."

"Yeah, everything is ok. Sylvia was just having a bad dream."

"Oh, dear. Hope she's ok."

"Yeah, she's fine and resting well now."

"So what is it? Did you open her gift?"

"Yeah," he smirked. "It's a free pass to a psychic reading."

"Oh, how cute! Imagine that—a professor of mathematics at a psychic reading."

"Yeah, well, what can I say?"

"That's funny. So how is she anyway? Still craving pizza every night?"

"There are the rare occasions when she'll request Hamburger Helper."

"Don't worry. She'll grow out of it eventually."

"I'll talk to you soon."

"Goodnight."

✵ ✵ ✵

On the corner of Pine and South, just beneath the railroad tracks, was a small shop with a frail neon business sign. The sign looked out of place, somewhat tarnished; the neon light faded in and out, changing from bright red to dimming purple. The sign vaguely read: *See Your Future.* Omar was hypnotized by the sign. He wondered whether he should attempt going in. He took a few steps back then remembered his promise to Sylvia. He looked again at the certificate making sure the address read the same as before. *This is it, I guess. What can it hurt?* He walked down the steps leading to the front door. Through the side window he saw a figure, someone sitting at a desk, waiting. Omar stood motionless feeling lost, void of thought. Then something came over him, a ghostly presence, something forceful and prying. Suddenly all of his past experiences raced through his mind, with every image projected to the sky and reeling across like a flock of black birds flying through a thin white cloud.

Omar opened the door to the sound of a dully chime. At the desk was an older man; his face pale, a nose slender, hooked like a hawk's beak.

"Can I help you?" the man asked.

"I'm sorry?"

"Are you here for a psychic reading?"

Omar was unsure and somewhat frightened. The room came into focus with large paisley red and gold curtains separating a back room. Candles illuminated from the corner, casting dancing shadows across tarot cards spread out on the waiting room table. Omar took a deep breath; the smell of patchouli oil curling up with the smoke of incenses. "Sir?" Omar looked up and saw the man staring at him.

"Oh, yes," Omar replied. "I have this gift certificate for a psychic reading."

"Gift certificate? I'm pretty sure we don't give those out. Can I see?"

Omar handed him the certificate. A gift certificate? Without taking his eyes off the card, the man entered through the red and gold curtains. A blade of green light beamed out from the back, but then quickly swallowed again by the curtains closing behind. Then Omar heard the sound of muffled words, the dampened pitch of questions and answers. Soon the curtains opened again, except no one showing, no one coming through—just the green light glowing, beckoning to enter. "Come in," a soft women's voice said. Omar cautiously walked towards the light. Behind the curtains was a small round table. Draped over the table was a silk cloth embroidered with gold threaded patterns of the zodiac. At center was a translucent crystal ball, a yellow haze swirled inside like a thousand angels trapped in a glass jar. Omar sat across from an empty chair and waited. Soon a lady entered. Her face blush-red, aqua-blue eyes; a maroon bandana worn tightly across her forehead.

"Your name is Omar, right?" she said, folding her hands on the table.

Omar thought for a moment.

"*Auh*, yes, Omar. But you must have gotten that from the certificate, right?"

"You have a daughter Sylvia?"

"Yes."

"And I take it she's the one who gave you the certificate?"

"Yeah, but I'm not sure how she got it."

"That's interesting."

"Why?"

"Well, *I* . . . just think it's nice that she would do something like that. Anyway, why don't we get started? I want you to take my hands and close your eyes."

Omar extended his hands across the table and felt the abnormally cold hands of the psychic. There was a sharp sting, the cold penetrated his hands and up into his arms. Like electricity, it ran through his veins, forcing him vulnerable and subdued.

Firmly gripping Omar's hands, the psychic inhaled through her nose and closed her eyes to the air above. The necromancy was now forming, the spirits circling above like a caressing whirlwind of cool air.

"You were born June 28th," the psychic proclaimed.

"Yes."

"That makes you a Cancer. Saturn is your planet."

"Saturn?"

"Yes *Saturn*," she responded quickly, as though trying to retain focus. "Saturn is arising strong, powerful like never before. Coming around, it takes energy and recycles it to you. It's something you'll soon discover . . . and it will change how you think—about what you've created, about what it is."

"I'm onto something I think," Omar said nervously. "I've been working on it for some time now and—"

"Yes, I see *it* now, coming clearer. Something you created or perhaps formulated, like chemistry or some type of reaction, a strong powerful reaction."

"I'm not quite finished with it yet. I still have some things to work out."

"No. You've already done it. Now it needs to come to you, so you'll know and see truly what has become."

Omar focused on the time. Seven years ago. Those laborious days at the university, the torpid and grueling hours put in. His past work, his submissions; that time so entranced and yet blurred by the enormous amount of work he accomplished while still teaching. And through it all only three or four manuscripts submitted to the International Mathematical Union.

"You will soon understand. Saturn will once again be closest to the earth in seven and half years."

Omar released his grip from the psychic, his hands instantly warming.

"Thank you for the reading, but I have to go. I'm running a little late."

"You have to pick up Sylvia."

Omar smirked. She was right to a certain extent: he generally waited for the bus to drop her off outside the house. It could be well assumed considering it was a school day, and the time was nearing three o'clock.

"Yes, I do."

"She's waiting for you."

✵ ✵ ✵

Sylvia was frightened.

The night sky had opened to a heavy down pour, the rain slashing down, pelting the roof like a thousand tap dancers dancing all at once. A thunderous roar shook the house as hollowed winds whistled past Sylvia's window. Omar entered the room and noticed Sylvia in bed holding the quilt over her eyes.

"It's ok," Omar said. "It's just a storm."

"Why is it so loud?" Sylvia said, peeking out from the quilt.

"Say," Omar quickly said to change the subject, "I noticed your new teacher's schedule ... so, why don't you tell me again what you guys are doing in October."

"I already told you," she grievously replied.

"I know. I'm sorry. You guys are making Halloween costumes, right?"

"Yeah, but I don't know what I'm gonna be yet," she said, as lightning flashed the room to bluish-white glow.

"Well, why not?"

"Cause you haven't told me."

"Cause I haven't told you? Sweetie, you can be whatever it is you want to be. Besides, it's a few months away so you'll have time to think about it. Come on, let's get some rest. I'll leave the door open, and I'll be right down the hall, ok?"

Sylvia nodded.

"Goodnight."

"Dad?"

"Yeah?"

"I counted the wrong number."

"What number?"

"The stars. There's only 1,634," Sylvia said, turning her head towards the telescope.

Omar tried to recall Sylvia's first count of the stars. 1,634?—Well, that's only one less than before. Curious by the difference, Omar looked through the telescope and tried to find focus. The rain continued to pour. Droplets of water slowly ran down the window, and through the scope, a small yellow spec—miniscule to the blackness, distorted, the yellow blurred, running like wet paint down the window. "Wait, that's it!" Omar said under his breath. "A window. That's what's missing. It all makes sense now."

"Dad?"

Omar turned away from the telescope, his eyes adjusting to Sylvia.

"Yeah?"

"Am I right?"

"About what?"

"1,634?"

"Oh, yes, precisely. Now what do you say we count some sheep now and get some rest, ok?"

"Ok, dad."

✳ ✳ ✳

Omar stood on the sidewalk outside his house and studied the large oak tree in his front yard. Some of the leaves were curling, changing colors, greens to yellows, yellows to bright oranges. He looked closely at the branches, the sunlight splintering through, blinding him as he considered the true nature of patterns. He thought about phylotaxonomy—the idea that every tree, every leaf, finds an unselfish way to share the light. It was all very profound, a mystery expressed by a simple equation, yet deeply buried in the answer of an irrational number. How can an irrational number be stabilized? Then the thought of Sylvia, her innocence, and how she had changed him, grounded him to realize the answer to his question. Through her window she had discovered more than just a sheer number. That night, in fact, she had inadvertently discovered the answer to Omar's question—that only through a window of time could an irrational number stabilized.

Omar was suddenly distracted from his thoughts by the sound of a van slowly approaching his driveway. The faces inside were familiar, but not immediately recognized. Soon the van slowed to a park. Omar realized it was Princeton's Department Head of Mathematics Professors James Loyer and his assistant Greg Bernstein. Omar was surprised to see them. He walked in their direction and greeted them with a concerned smile.

"So to what do I owe this unexpected honor?" Omar asked.

"We wanted to congratulate you first hand," Professor Loyer responded. "We've just found out that you've been nominated for a Fields Medal."

"A Fields Medal? You guys are joking, right?"

"Absolutely not. The board of directors has accepted one of your theorems."

Omar stood speechless as he thought about the profound implications.

"They feel it can be applied to new applications in number theory," Bernstein added.

"Which theorem?" Omar finally asked.

"Sylvia's Window Theorem," Loyer said. "We'll see you in Berlin next month for the announcements. We've got our fingers crossed on this one."

"I can't believe it."

Professor Loyer patted Omar on the shoulder. "Believe it. It's real. And remember, always transpire suum pectus mundoque," Loyer said as he and Bernstein walked back to the van. It took Omar a few seconds to recognize the words. He had heard or seen them before, somewhere.

"Wait!" Omar yelled, running to Professor Loyer's side. "What does that mean?"

"It's Latin. It means to rise above oneself and grasp the world. It's engraved on all the Fields Medals."

Omar watched a subtle gust of wind move a small tornado of leaves across the yard. He looked back and noticed the van moving slowly in the distance. It soon disappeared through a thick fog. Minutes passed as he thought about the theorem, the intricacies and confounding details—the convoluted theory so difficult to hold in his mind. Something was missing, he thought. Soon through the haze emerged a school bus. The playful chattering of children, all dressed in Halloween costumes, arriving just in front of the house. The harsh diesel engine fluttered out to screeching breaks. The double doors quickly swung open to reveal an exuberant Spiderman jumping off the last step with web-casting wrists pointed at a branch on the oak tree. Close behind were Batman and Dracula; their capes flapping as they ran the sidewalks back home. Then came

Sylvia—her face powdered white and dressed in a blue shimmering caftan with runic characters running down the sleeves. She wore a green silk headband and a gold necklace holding a blue topaz gem.

"Wow, look at you!" Omar exclaimed. "What are you suppose to be?"

"You should know, dad," she said in a disappointing tone.

"Are you an Elephant?"

"No!"

"Are *you* ... *a* ... Tiger?"

"No, Dad!"

"Well, then, what are you?"

"I'm not telling you."

"Can I still have a few more guesses?"

"Dad?"

"Yeah, sweetie?"

"What's for dinner?"

Omar thought for a second, then looked steadily into Sylvia's eyes.

"Well," he said in a suggestive tone, "why don't you tell me?"

Sylvia gazed back, her eyes transfixed, a face uncompromised to Omar's penetrating stare.

"*Emmm ... are we ... having ...* PIZZA!"

Omar quickly lifted Sylvia off her feet and playfully swung her through the air.

"How did you know we're having pizza!"

"Cause I'm psychic!" she yelled through her laughter. "Cause I'm psychic!"

Omar set Sylvia back on her feet.

"So, if you're psychic, where's your crystal ball?"

"I gave it to someone, as a present."

"Boy, you're just full of presents. Why did you give it away?"

Sylvia looked up to the sky as though searching for a lost angel.

"Because she's leaving now. She said she'll give it back, once she comes around again. Dad, promise we'll wait for her?"

Omar knelt to Sylvia and gave her a hug.

"I promise. We will be here when she comes back. In the meantime, do you want to go to Berlin?"

"So you can pick up your medal?"

"Well that was quick."

"I'm sorry. I won't do it again."

"That's quite alright, precious. Come on. Let's have some pizza."

✦ ✦ ✦

A VIEW FROM A DISTANT BALCONY

A View from a Distant Balcony

I walked in 5 minutes late to a classroom filled with students. Professor Lucus had yet to arrive. He had a tendency to keep the students waiting. I took a seat in the back corner and opened my notebook. Only the date and one line of words:

"Sept30th,
  Generation Y is on its own axis."

Professor Lucus entered precisely 12 minutes late. He paced around the island lecture table; his eyes transfixed to the floor. The muffled classroom voices drew silent. Lucus' face crimped up to the pain of a lost thought. Up. The ceiling, searching.

"I have a simple confession," he finally said. "I must say, and for the sole purpose of today's class and for all you hard working students, who—in your greatest of hopes and dreams—will most certainly carry on from this great university. As it were a long time ago, I was employed as a garbage man in Chicago. I would have to get up early, about 4 or so, and go around town picking up garbage. No big deal. Just go out, get the shit, and come back. That's all. I did that. I did that for awhile, those early mornings. That was before I followed up with my education and became a history professor. A professor?—still sorta sounds funny to me when I say that. I had a classmate, a friend of mine back then, who turned into one big hive over it all. He got sick with these enormous red blisters—just broke down, malfunctioned and missed the test. He was the smartest person I knew at the time … but he just got too worked up. And all it was in the end was us sitting in a room for 6 hours writing everything we knew about it, the subject that is. Then we made it. I didn't give a shit to be honest. If I failed, then so what. I'd try again—or maybe just go back picking up garbage. But to my friend it was everything, nothing meant more to him. So here

I am with a story to tell, up front in a room filled with students, and I worry sometimes about what some of you might think, about whether you'll make it out to be something more than what it truly is. I hope this class will teach you something outside the curriculum. It's important to know that you have to get out and experience the world in order to understand how it works, you see. Because if you do finish up with your college—and I hope you all do—then you're going to have a piece of paper that qualifies you for it. Just, please—please don't be a fucking garbage man."

HA, HA, HA, HA, HA, HA, HA…

"I'm only trying to say that you need to get out and play with the world a bit, rub your nose in it. It will get you down and mess with your head, but that's what gives you that sense. And sometimes it's not the text that awakens you. Sometimes it's talking to the people who were actually there, the old-timers—see what they say. Because after all, they were there for Christ's sake."

Professor Lucus made it into an assignment. Every student was instructed to interview a veteran from World War II and type up a report by the following Wednesday. I didn't have a choice. I knew no one from the war. The American Legion would have to be my stop. I had walked past the Legion on several occasions only to glance in and see the silhouettes moving across a dim, smoky room. I had always been curious about the shadows. I made plans to visit them tomorrow.

✲ ✲ ✲

I arrived hesitant to Enter. The place didn't feel right. I stood in the parking lot staring at the bar. I wasn't sure what I was doing, just there—waiting like a child. I double checked my pack for pens and paper. I went back to my car and put in a cd. Nine Inch Nails. Year Zero.

I got my violence in high def ultra-realism! . . . All a part of this [fucked up] nation!
I got my fist, I got my [pen], I got survivalism!

The song pierced. I'm ready. It's time! Reznor please! Start the revolution! I'm on my knees, begging. I've only been on my knees 5 times and that was only for God. Down to Mexico I'll move. They'll know me: The Great Jamison Loft!

Revolutionary! Prophet of the People! I'll set the canons, direct course. San Diego. You just say the word. Start your song. This is our time!

I pushed stop. Quite. Alone.

My aggression and delusions slowly faded with the silence.

I walked into the A.L. noticing 3 Veterans drinking at the bar. One of the Veterans looked extremely old and fragile, his back crimpled, hunched over to a network of thinning blue veins. His mouth gapped open, drooling a small puddle of saliva on the bar. The bartender was an older lady, wrinkled skin that drooped soft layers around the mouth. She had pure white hair curled short, a white towel draped around her shoulder.

"Whut'll we be havin?" she asked.

"Do you have any raspberry coolers?"

"I'm sorry. I'm gonna hav'ta ask you for some id."

"Sure."

"I can never tell these days," she said while slowly putting her glasses on. "As you get older you start to lose track. You said Coors?"

"Coors will be fine."

I took a seat at the bar and scanned the room. A standard dive bar with a pool table, jukebox, and a tv mounted at the end of the bar. There was a low, unclear admixture of sound as the jukebox played in unison with the tv. I looked at the veterans sitting at the bar. One of them seemed to be the leader. He was little bigger than the other two, his face a little less aged. He sat there and the aura of respect somehow surrounded him. It felt necessary to wait before speaking. There was time needed, time to gage me, to sense who I was.

The front door opened. A blade of light cut across the room. A guy in his 40's, long hair, long nose, a thin mustache. He had wide-eyes and a joker smile. He sat two seats from me, the tv above his head. I immediately had a feeling he was going to cause trouble. He ordered a beer then looked around the room. He was suddenly taken by the Budweiser poster on the wall. A beautiful brunet holding a foamy beer, calling to the consumer: Take this beer and you'll have a good chance at landing me for the night.

"Wooooh, look at that!" he said, pointing at the poster. "Look at that! That's what I'm talking about, that ass! Ha, Ha, Ha, Ha, Hee, Hee! She's got an ass on her! Big hips, but hey, I can handle it! Ha, Ha, Ha, Ha, Ha! That's valuable property. That'll take care of you until you're 50, until your hair turns gray, man!"

"Maybe you should ask her out," I said.

"I should! I'm forty-years old! She'd prauyee have too much energy for me, but I don't care! You know what I like are those Asian women! Woooh, they have it! Ha, Ha, Ha! Nowadays you can actually order one out of a magazine!"

"Valuable property out of magazine?"

"Yeah, yeah, I've seen it happen! I'm forty-years old, but that doesn't stop me from being a horny dog! Ha, Ha, Ha, Ha, Ha, Hee, Hee... Hey!—you remember Tonya Hard-on? Tonya Hard-on?

"The figure skater?"

"Yeah. Tonya Hard-on! HA, HA, Ha, ha, hee. She was little ... PETITE! Had that nice little firm body. *Emmm*, with those tight black pants."

I suddenly realized that Ben was periodically looking up at the tv. It seemed as though he was becoming increasingly distracted by it.

"I'd like that! HA, HA, HA, HA, HA! Where are you from? My name is Ben by the way. I can tell you're a traveling man like myself. But you know what? I have to tell ya. You're not going to find people like us around. People aren't like us—they hang out in groups, not travelers like ourselves. They look at us sitting here by ourselves and laugh. They think we're outcasts, losers because we don't fit in. HA, HA, HE, HE, HA, HA! But that's it. You can't be by yourself. Now you're a weirdo or something. I've traveled around the states, all up and down the coast, but you know what? I've never found humanity. It's never there. You can go to Europe and you're not going to find humanity. But I tell you what, you sure can go to Asia and find an Asian woman! HA, HA, HA, HA, HA, HA, HA, HEE, HEEE! They'll take care of you until your 50, until your hair turns gray, man!"

Again distracted by the tv, Ben propped himself up on the barstool. Lifting up from his knees, he stood wobbly as he pushed a button on the tv. It went silent only for a second before a loud static ROAR burst across the room. Startled by the noise, Ben slipped off his chair, hitting his head on the bar before falling to the ground.

"GOD DAMN! TURN THAT THING DOWN!" one of the veterans yelled.

Ben quickly got up from the floor and propped himself up on the stool. He managed to balance himself just enough to randomly push another button. Fortunately, it was the mute button. A silent screen of black and white allowed Neil Young to come in clear from the jukebox.

"You see," Ben said, "Neil Young. We all like Neil Young. I just wanted to make sure everyone could hear it."

The veterans looked extremely agitated. I knew it was going to be a difficult interview. As much as I couldn't stand the guy, I was now guilty by association. I waited and prayed for Ben to leave. I was on my third beer when Ben got up to use the restroom. I thought it would be good time, maybe the only time to ask. I sat in the seat next to the lead veteran.

"Excuse me, sir?"

"Yeah?"

"Were you in WWII?"

"What do you know about war?" he said.

"I'm sorry, sir. I won't bother you."

I grabbed my pack and walked out the front door. Outside I noticed the sky was orange, a sunset casting a pinkish glow on the horizon. I stood and watched the birds circle through the clouds. I thought about the war, how it must of been. Millions of people dead. Then the door opened behind me. Neil Young's number one fan approached me.

"Hey, buddy," he said. "You think I can ask you for a favor?"

"Yeah, sure," I said despairingly.

"Do you think I can get an extra smoke from you?"

I gave him a cigarette.

"I thought I was in for it back there," he said.

"Yeah, they seem pretty grumpy."

"Say, thanks. I actually got a train to catch. I'm a traveling man like yourself."

"Happy trails."

I watched Ben walk off, periodically kicking stones across his path. I stood alone wondering where to go next. I had only two days before the assignment. I was almost to my car when I heard a voice.

"Hey, kid."

I looked behind me; it was the lead veteran.

"Yes, sir?" I said, anxiously trotting towards him.

"What brings you here?"

"I'm a student. I have an assignment to interview someone from the war."

"A student, huh?"

"Yeah, I'm taking a history class."

"What part of the war are you studying?"

"No particular part, really."

"Well, why don't you come in ... I'll buy you a raspberry cooler."

We entered the bar. The jukebox was silent. It seemed as though the place was waiting for us. I sat next to him at the bar and opened my notebook. He introduced himself as John Walsh. I was memorized by the sound of his voice. It was hypnotic, words spoken deep and slow. He spoke about the politics surrounding the war, about his platoon and their mission. Then I asked the most general question possible: "What was it like?" He took a deep breath. He was caught in a whirlwind of the scattered thoughts. He took a sip of his beer and looked straight ahead.

"At the time I don't think anyone could have put it into words. We were all committed, submerged to something difficult to explain. Yet all of us felt, and all of us knew, that we were in that place and time for something more. We could just feel it, something there. Nowadays people view the war only taking in the images of destruction. We see on television the pain, people dying on the battlefields, people starving to death in the concentration camps, and this is not to be taken lightly, mind you. But underneath it all, underneath the rummage of dying men and burning buildings, was this powerful force, this energy of love; it was just there— sheltered, waiting patiently. It seemed as if everything was suddenly put on hold, temporarily dormant you might say. And, of course, it was hard for us to see or feel it at the time because we were all amerced in something dreadful. With every inch of our soul, we held on tight to that one photo of our precious girl back home, and prayed that one day we might see her again. It was a shared commonality among us. We were all there together going through the same experience, so naturally we bonded as One. Soon the sadness of the war ended and love came to the surface so powerful you can't even begin to imagine. This is what people miss and wonder about the war. You see, those men who died ... those great men we honor, not only sacrificed themselves for their country, they sacrificed themselves for a lost love."

I wasn't sure what to say. I was overwhelmed. I sat there trying to find the proper words. This man—veteran of a great war, crystal blue eyes that instantly penetrated the soul; rugged face of wire-scarred skin—spoke of love. And pain, sacrifice. Agony. Despair. I hadn't realized that underneath the hard faces were men still holding on.

Mr. Walsh looked at me as I sat motionless. I saw his concern. He wondered what I would make of it, if I could truly understand. Could I take what he said and actually internalize it, put it into some constructive form? Or was I just another person of our modern times who has become trapped under the Image of the bright and illusive screen.

I drove home and felt the bitterness of the working class. All of them up high in corporate buildings, looking down with splints in their third eyes. They only hoped to hurry home and watch a parody of their sad lives. A primetime escape not even worthy of the drug. Work to consume. That's it. Never thought twice about finding a medium to create or express their repressed souls.

I turned on the radio. Billy Joel's *We Didn't Start the Fire*. It furthered Walsh's point. I realized then that we are still here tasting Baby-boomer pre-cum. The so-called 60's, a bunch of clowns in their little tie-died outfits, prancing around on acid, rebelling in their nakedness. But where are they now in these sad times? They must of hung-up their tie-died shirts a long time ago. Tap more oil, take more money, and let the Cialis dissolve on your tongue as you watch the polar ice caps melt away. Never mind health care, hurricanes, mortgage crisis, social security, national debt. You've got the SUV with the DVD in the back. You've got yours. Why rebel now? You would only be rebelling against yourself, the security of the nation—same thing you rebelled against in the 60's. You didn't start the fire, but you're doing a great job perpetuating it.

X, we've been silent for too long.

X, torched and lost.

Continually bounded by careful sculptures of a Divorced past.

Rise.

Vision.

X.

Escape the screen.

Hold the pen.

23.5 degrees.

And let it come.

Now it's our time.

I got home and turned on the computer. I began typing.

"*. . . The so-called Greatest Generation went to war, many of them returning home to attend college and open up successful businesses. They wanted peace and security, a soothing calmness across a great land. They knew the repercussions of the WWI, the failure of the 14 Points. They would do their best to extinguish any notion of another world war. And there were a lot of good soldiers who died in Vietnam, he said—and how we supposedly "lost" the war, how it was a "pointless" war, how the soldiers returned home unaccepted as "heroes." What if Vietnam didn't happen? I guess 1's and 0's are the only numbers. 14 points? 14 shades of gray? Sheltered little hippies—so safe in their upbringing never felt the threat of a little Tsar bomb. Now the Boomers* *have control, and it's Iraq, Iran, and the spread of terrorist. I wouldn't think you're going to label terrorism a paranoia anytime soon...."*

I stopped there. I realized I didn't know enough about the overall history, nor was I actually there to sense and find my own perspective. I was naïve and emotional. Dangerous combination for writing. I never returned to the paper. I dropped out of school and made plans for Mexico.

12 STEPS TO MEXICO

It was forced to a promise.

I sat across from Professor Lucus and took note of his self-managed hair-cut. It appeared as though he was just cutting snippets away from his wide, circular eyes; the rest was busy with spilt-ends, especially in the back and around the ears. Having been a hippie from the 60's, Lucus still maintained the freedom vibe. Smoking pot was a given, but I sometimes wondered if he still took acid. His pupils were permanently dilated, looking as if he never got off the Magic Bus. On the side, he taught history and volunteered his time as a rehab counselor.

"So how are things going?" he asked.

"They're going, I guess."

"Is everything ok?"

"Yeah, I suppose."

"So, what can you tell me about last week?"

"Last week? What about it?"

"I mean, did you experience anything that made you upset, or possibly sway your decision to drop out of school?"

I knew prior to showing up he'd ask this question, even predicted a few of the exact words. In any case, I was still left off-guard. To be honest, I didn't know why, nor did I care to reflect on my decision. I just knew I had to do it— at least temporarily.

"I don't know," I said. "I guess lately I've been feeling these strange vibes, like something tugging at me, something outside this whole thing. It's almost like this force trying to guide me somewhere."

"Deep inside is there some place you feel you might want to go?"

"I just want to move in a positive direction, I guess. But it's weird. Sometimes I want to be away from everything."

Professor Lucus sat up in his chair. "Away from everything?" he asked in a concerning tone.

"No, it's not like that. I mean, it's more like wanting peace."

"Peace?"

"I'm not sure how to explain it sometimes. I remember once when I was younger my parents checked us into a fancy hotel in Chicago. We were on one of the very top floors, way up where you could almost see everything. Later that night my parents went out for a conference or something, and I was left alone in the room. I remember looking out the window and watching all the cars pass by, the headlights just moving along slowly over the bridge and down the highway. It was like watching a trail of glowing ants or something, just moving along. I watched it for hours, feeling peace and this comfort, like tranquility. Somehow it made me relax and not think all the time—just those cars in the dark going somewhere nobody knew."

"Sounds like you're happier behind the scenes, so-to-speak. Unfortunately, sometimes you can't really escape it."

"I could minimize it if I had enough money. Everyone thought Howard Hughes went insane towards the end. He was just sick of all the bullshit. When a conversation filled the room, he couldn't listen. Because ninety-nine percent of it was bullshit. Didn't matter if it was Einstein talking to Bohr or Jim Steward talking to Elvis. To him, it was all bullshit."

"I guess you're right to an extent. Elvis was full-of-shit."

"Literally."

"Look, Jamison, next semester I want you to consider taking my class, Perspectives on History. It seems to go along with some of the things we're talking about. It may help you see things from a different angle."

"Perspectives on History? Can I ask you a question?"

"Anything."

"Who do you think has a better ass, Meg Ryan or J-Lo?"

"Well, that's easy. Meg Ryan, for sure."

"Now that's bullshit."

"She's just better. J-Lo's ass is too big."

"See, this is what I'm talking about. This is why I'm going to lock myself away and piss in little tiny milk bottles."

I got up from my chair and began to walk out. I didn't want to seem rude, but I was going to be late meeting up with my ride to Mexico. Besides, I had spoken how I felt and didn't have much more to offer.

"I want to see you in my class, Jamie," he said sternly. "And remember I still have those rehab sessions. You're always welcome to attend if you feel you need to."

✣ ✣ ✣

It was summer, though you could sense fall slowly setting in. The nights were coming sooner and the ocean air was stronger. I thought about the city of San Diego, thought about how it would be a great place to grow up—with the beach, warm weather, and close proximity to Mexico. And then I remembered someone once telling me that devil himself often takes his vacations in a small town called Tijuana. A place where the good-hearted souls are violently preyed upon, the shit-stained streets, the withered storefronts—all there functioning in this desperate haven for corruption and greed.

We were riding in a convertible. Big Curls was driving. He said something about his uncle loaning him the car. Curls had been my Irish friend since we were 7. He was nick-named Big Curls early on in elementary school. Back then the boys on the playground always made fun of his red afro. The girls, however, often begged to touch it. Just once, they'd say. They thought it felt good on their hands; it was like a soft sponge or something. When Curls refused, they'd sneak up behind him and quickly pat him on the back of the head. I had always thought he took the girls the wrong way. To me, it seemed like flirtatious gesturing; but for him, it was just another demeaning sign against his look. He tried everything to tame the unmanageable afro, even tried shaving it. The day he came to class with a shaved head was the worst. His ears stuck out beyond what everyone could imagine, and then it was "Dumbo" for the next 6 weeks.

Barely out of San Diego, I could see Mexico—or at least I thought it was Mexico. The landscape looked different, more bland and rocky, like it had been horribly excavated into clumps of pale dirt. In next lane over was a car staying in lane with its blinker on.

"Is that idiot going to merge or what?" Big Curls asked.

"He's probably waiting for you to get out of his blind spot."

"He's the blind one, not me. So how was your time with Lucus?"

"He mentioned something about going to his rehab sessions."

"Again? Are you serious?"

"Yeah, I think he's just concerned."

"You know what bothers me the most about rehab?"

"No, what?"

"It's these people. All of them convincing themselves that the drug is the bad guy. The drug doesn't appreciate that kind of behavior, Jamison. But they don't realize. They just go on blaming their sober problems on the drug, pointing the finger, always needing something to blame. I like to add a little of my own terminology and call it reverse denial. Their problems exist no matter what. They stop drinking thinking it'll salvage their depression, then realizing they're fucked up anyway, they decide to go on a binge and cry, *but I'm an alcoholic, but I'm an alcoholic!* No you're not, damn it! You're an abuser! And it doesn't matter what you abuse, you're still the one who decides to turn your back on a potential good friend. Now it's your enemy and, even worse, an excuse for your fucked up situation."

"Wow, sounds like you should be the one doing the counseling."

"Nah, they'd never get it."

We approached the border terminal. My eyes began to burn. I felt nervous, anxiously awake. On the other side was a haunting reminder: a long line of cars at check point, waiting to get back into the states. There were patrol agents, k-9s, cars pulled off to the side, searchlights and sirens, guns, rules—expectations.

"Don't worry, I've got a plan," Big Curls said, trying to comfort my nerves.

"I've been caught before doing this shit before," I said. "If it happens again, I'm screwed."

"You're already screwed, Jamison. We're all screwed. Don't worry."

"I can worry, alright! Those guys are fucking professionals; they know when you're hiding something!"

"Shit, they're like cops," he said, shrugging me off.

"No, they're not like cops. See, that's where you're wrong. They're more than that. They take harder tests than cops do, they know like five different languages. Some of them have lie detector tests embedded in their brains. I know this. I've seen it."

"Hey, keep your cool. Look at you all worked up. No wonder you got caught acting like this. Calm down."

"You better have a plan."

"You don't even know."

Instantly the rules changed. We had crossed the border without any questions from the authorities. We were now in the land of sleeping greed, smelling stagnant air comprised mostly of a strong admixture of sewer and petroleum. The decrepit roads sinuously paved in and out until finally merging to a single road downtown. Lining the street were hustling beggars, malnourished dogs, little pop-belly kids with no shoes and thinning undersized shirts. The frail store fronts lacked foundation, some partially crumbled like broken card castles. Nevertheless, you could still see the purpose of it all: the defunct structure of a lawless and exploitive financial district. It was dry-hump commerce at its finest, and it scared anyone who knew the true nature of it.

Our first destination was the doctor's office. As we walked in, the floors whistled and groaned. A disturbing sound—almost torturous, like that of a distressed murmur heard from the grave of a lost man. Inside were two floor fans rotating slowly, causing the flies to erratically swarm through the circulating air. Soon a beautiful Mexican secretary greeted us. She wore a white blouse that exposed the top half of her breasts. The sweat on her brown skin caused a sensual glint off her body. I was instantly infatuated. I heard the cocking of a fan. It turned at the right moment. A rush of cool air skimmed across her face, blowing her black curly hair away from her soft cheek.

"Can I help you," she said in a strong Spanish accent.

"We were hoping to see the doctor for some medicine," Big Curls responded.

"Right this way."

She led us back to the doctor's office. I entered noticing an older man sitting behind a desk. Behind him was a wall displaying his medical certifications—all framed, signed and stamped. It proved him reputable and it hit me then. I had to talk to Big Curls before we started. I tapped him on the shoulder and signaled him to meet in the corner of the room. Curls approached me with a frustrated look.

"What's going on here?" he said.

"I've got an idea."

"What now?"

"Why not forge something like this?"

"Forge what? What the hell are you talking about? We haven't got the goods yet and you're already trippin."

"No listen," I spoke in a frantic, loud whisper. "It's perfect. Why not actually be the doctor in Tijuana? Cut the middle man out, right? Think about it. We could have our own beautiful secretary—just like this guy. She'll be there, you know, scratching the back of our necks with those long fingernails, rubbing our shoulders, helping us with the paper work. That is, of course, after we have our early afternoon siesta—a little lunch and percodan around 11. Right? Then it's back to work supplying the menopausal women with their paxil. Of course, the geriatric sinners will need their antibiotics and the kids will need their codeine. But that's it! And there's our money, Curls! Simple! Genius!

And we'll have it all at our disposal. Then a little traffic at the border, and back home to the wife and kids—all of them there just waiting in a beautiful house perched against the American ocean."

"Wow, that secretary has gotten you all worked up. Look at you. You can't even think straight."

"What are you talking about? It's a good idea."

"Alright, alright, hold on for just one second. Let me tell you something before you get too carried away with this drug-induced utopian idea."

"What? You can't tell me it's not a good idea."

"The pursuit of happiness comes in many different forms, Jamison. See how our *wants* somehow, suddenly, turn into our *needs*? At one point we all looked up to the fancy stuff: the cable tv, the microwaves and dishwashers, new cars and new computers; but it was all too expensive, beyond our reason for consumption; that is until the upper-class overproduced it. Then it was all spoon-fed graciously to the lower-class. And the lower-class fought over it, stepping on each other to get it first. There was actually a Walmart security guard that was trampled to death on black Friday. Remember? And all of this because why? Don't you remember our little saying? You can't enter the secret fort unless...?"

"It makes sense though," I insisted.

"Come on. Unless...?"

"I know, I know," I finally gave in.

"Unless you *have*...?"

"The new action Skywalker," I reluctantly said.

"That's right, amigo! The new action Luke Skywalker figure," he said, grabbing me by the shoulders. "You know this, remember? Now let's not get worked up by those above us trying to exploit us to social jealousy. We're here for one thing, Jamie. Come on. Let's go see the blessed doctor."

He was right. My hormones were running out of control. The secretary had me by the emotional balls, and like an acid trip, I was thinking beyond my mental capacity. I calmed myself and followed Big Curls to the doctor's desk.

"So, what is it you like?" the doctor asked.

"We are in the market for oxycontins," Big Curls said.

"*Ahh, yes, yes.* I see. Oxycontins. Yes, how many you like?"

"Seventeen bottles."

"*Yes, yes,* my friend. That'll be 25 for each prescription."

Big Curls put the money on the desk as the doctor filled out the prescription slips. We made the exchange and shook the doctor's hand. On our way out, I engaged in a lasting look with the secretary. She smiled back as if she knew what I was thinking. I wanted to talk to her, just to see how she'd react to my words. It didn't matter if it was good or bad—just a flinch or a wink would suffice. I decided to approach her. My heart began to race and I completely stopped breathing. I looked into her eyes and said, "In the end, everything fills to a new beauty." I didn't know where it came from. I just said it. It was surreal. Suddenly, I heard a loud burst of laughter from behind me. The laughter brought me back to reality, sobered me up enough to know that what I said was completely ludicrous. I looked back and noticed Big Curls on one knee laughing while trying to hold himself up on the door knob. I looked back at the secretary. She smiled, then looked down at her desk.

We were walking as fast as we could without looking suspicious. The beggars at storefronts were sometimes rancorous; they wanted your money, your life, your opportunities, and they would often beg for it. They tried to sell you on their sorrow and grief, and if that didn't work, they'd sometimes become aggressive. I quickly learned not look anyone in the eyes. The second you made eye contact it was over. Soon they'd be at your feet with poorly hand-crafted jewelry or some type of wood carving. Curls didn't seem to care. A few people approached him and he quickly walked right past.

We finished up at the pharmacia and headed towards *Hotel Sanchez*. I started thinking about the drug, its effects on body and mind. The one thing I didn't like about oxycontins is that it made you pleasantly naïve. You could be balls-deep in a donkey, feverishly humping away, while perverted tourist snapped your picture—and you'd smile for the camera as if nothing was happening. Because nothing could go wrong when you're high and happy on pills. It's similar to Winona Ryder's episode at *Saks Fifth Avenue*. There are only two—binary or perhaps intertwining—reasons why a wealthy actress would steal: either she's a kleptomaniac or she's high on pills. And, of course, we shouldn't discount the fact that there might be the synergy of both reasons. Pills, in conjunction with a subtle, yet, faulty personality, will undoubtedly bring everything out. It's an inordinate feeling of pleasure that most people can't handle. Many drown in it, and the next thing they know, they're stealing or raping, or being raped, or beaten, or killed in a car accident.

We were about a block away from the hotel when Big Curls stopped in his tracks and snapped his fingers. "Wait!" he said. "I almost forgot." We suddenly took a sharp turn into a narrow, almost hidden alleyway. "Come on. We need one more thing." Lining the alley were little makeshift shops selling beads, necklaces, blankets, and Mexican flags. Above, hanging from the top of the buildings, were colorful piñatas swaying in the breeze. Curls eventually found a stand selling maracas. He approached the seller and bargained him down to four maracas for two American dollars.

✧ ✧ ✧

We checked into our room at *Hotel Sanchez*. The room was stale and shoddy, the light green carpet stained and worn. The tv was small and old with only three channels—all of which were Spanish-speaking. Outside the window, across the street, was a two-story bar catering to people having a late afternoon margarita.

Big Curls opened a bottle of oxycontin. He had a stern look on his face. He looked at me and told me to sit down on the bed. I suddenly felt like I was a curious virgin about to be taught a valuable lesson in life.

"Ok. Do you know how we administer?" he asked.

"It's a pill. You just take it down."

"No, no, no, no, amigo. It's definitely not like that at all."

"Then what then?"

"This has a pernicious beauty, my friend," he said, holding the pill out like it was an engagement ring. "These are 80 milligram oxycontins. You don't want to mess this up."

"Alright already. Then what's the method?"

"First things first, amigo. What's this called?"

I was growing extremely intolerant to his *need* to call me amigo.

"It's a fucking pain killer!" I lashed out. "What's the big deal?"

"Yeah, but what kind of pain killer? See, this is where semantics and linguistics comes in, root words and shit."

"They teach you this in rehab?"

"So say it. What's this called?"

"Oxycontin."

"Say it slow. Use the syllables."

"Oxy ... con ... tin."

"And so oxy?"

"Probably short for oxycodone."

"Good, Poncho! Right! But now here's the important part. Go on."

"Contin. Probably...?"

"Come on."

"Can we take the fucking thing already?"

"Contin, my friend—or in other words, time released, eh. It's specially coated, layered, you know. Kicks in every two hours ... *unless* ... you chew it up. Then you break the chastity belt and everything becomes yours *all at once*."

He handed me a pill. I chewed it up. Then an eye-squinting taste, so strong I could barely keep it in my mouth. It was like extra strength aspirin dosed with a tinge of battery acid, first on the surface of my tongue, then to the blood stream and beneath. As the sting came, I felt my body loosen away from the parasitic stress, my tongue curled against the bitter taste, my vision blurred by a fountain of tears, and the instant disregard for all pain and suffering came as I felt overwhelmed with emotion. I stumbled to the window and held myself up by the curtain. I looked outside and saw the sun setting on the ocean horizon. The sunlight was bright, more intense; it scraped across the atmosphere refracting into rays of nuclear orange, then coming to the surface, it spread pink through a haze of thin dust. Suddenly, under the sentiment of the drug, I went into deep thought on how I could be a great marriage counselor.

"What do you say we take a venture around the block," I said, noticing my voice had become soft and concerning.

"To where?"

"Maybe there's a play going on somewhere."

"A play? Are you crazy?"

"Shit, I don't know," I said. "Let's just get out, let the breeze take us where it may."

"I feel too relaxed. I feel like I'm swimming without all the movement or something."

"I know, but we're only here for one night."

Big Curls took out the rest of the pills and set them on the table. He then intently stared at the maracas as though analyzing them for acute operation. He grabbed one of the handles and began forcefully bending it back.

"HEY! DON'T BREAK THAT!" I yelled.

He calmly turned to me, releasing his grip, showing an innocent hand across the air.

"Do you want to wind up in prison for ten years?" he said.

"No."

"Then chill."

Again, he grabbed the handle, but then paused. It seemed he had a new idea. He turned the maraca around. Now holding the round bulb, he slammed the handle on the table breaking it flush. My ears were too hypersensitive to keep a straight face. I heard a loud crash. The beads fell out across the table and onto carpet. I heard the sound of large thumps, like hail falling from the sky. He shook out the remaining beads, then funneled a hand full of oxycontins into the bulb.

"They'll never catch this one," he said, pulling a small bottle of wood glue from his shirt pocket. "Now we just wood glue them back together and wait for them to dry."

I couldn't believe my eyes. It was ingenuity at its finest.

"Wow, who taught you about that?" I asked.

"Nobody. I was watching MacGyver and he did something similar, only it was with a tooth pick, a napkin, and a razor. So naturally I took the idea and applied it to real life."

"You should win a Nobel Peace Prize for this."

"Nah, they'd never get it."

✵ ✵ ✵

It was now dark outside and Curls had made up his mind to stay at the hotel. The second I walked outside I was intrigued by the lifelessness. The streets were pretty much empty, only a cool breeze crossing my face and the movement of newspapers swirling through the streets. I looked up to the bar across the street and saw four people left drinking. I suddenly felt out of breath and took a seat on a bench. Every nerve in my body was vibrating, and I was itching myself erratically, especially on the tip of my nose. I began to hallucinate a small squirrel on a tree stump; it stood still, looking at me, perfectly poised upright on hind legs. It seemed like hours went by, the two of us locked in stare. Finally, I heard the hint of music from down the street. It somehow beckoned me. I sought after it like an insect following a pheromone trail.

I eventually approached the origin of music and realized that I stumbled upon a strip club. As I walked in, I noticed no one, just loud music and laser lights flashing across an empty stage. I took a seat at the bar and waited. Soon two strippers followed a man through red curtains. The girls took the stage and the man took my order.

"I'll have a Pacifico, please."

"You like the girls?" he said, handing me a beer.

"Yeah, they're beautiful."

"I've got something better for you, my friend."

"That's ok. I need some ones for the dancers."

"For them?" he said, pointing to the strippers. "No good. You come with me."

"No that's alright. I'm fine."

He handed me the change from the beer which included some ones. I went up to the stage and tipped one of the strippers through her g-string. When

I returned to the bar, I noticed the bartender looked extremely agitated. He had a pronounced asymmetrical mustache which looked even more off-centered with his grin.

"You wait here!" he said, leaving back through the red curtains.

I waited, watched the dancers, the laser lights beaming through their black hair. I kept itching myself, my nose turning red. Suddenly someone vehemently tapped me on the shoulder. I looked behind me and the bartender was standing next to another man wearing a silver police badge. "You come with us," said the man with the badge. He grabbed my arm and pulled me away from the seat. My first instinct was to swing, but I instantly remembered my thoughts from before: I couldn't afford to be pleasantly naïve and wind up in jail, or raped, or stolen from. I would go with the flow, do as they said, and hopefully, somehow, work my way out.

They guided me back through the red curtains to an alleyway behind the club. The alley was dimly lit blue from a neon insect zapper hanging from a rafter above. Lining a brick wall were a dozen or more strung-out prostitutes. They were extremely impatient, pacing side-to-side, itching themselves in need for the drug.

"I help you find," the bartender said. He walked over to one of the more truculent, overweight prostitutes. "You like this one?"

"Auh, maybe," I said.

"You go ahead. Pick for yourself."

Shrouded behind one of the more aggressive prostitutes, was a younger, innocent looking girl. She had a skinny figure, straight black hair, and seemed to be trapped emotionally in some type of stupor. A part of me felt sorry for her. She seemed out of place amongst the rest of the girls; she stayed back, almost shy-like and fragile. I approached her, leaned close to her ear and whispered: "Don't worry. I'll take care of it." I turned around and walked over to the bartender. "I'll take the one in the back."

The bartender escorted us a few blocks down to a run-down brothel. Inside was a large man sitting at a desk. The bartender approached him and a private conversation ensued. I was soon called over and asked to pay 40-dollars. I paid the man at the desk and then found myself locked in arms with the prostitute. We were guided down a long hallway to an adjacent room. With the exception of a twin size bed, the room was completely empty of furniture. The door was shut behind us. The prostitute immediately took her shirt off, then her skirt and underwear, then laid on the bed and spread her arms out.

"Fuck me," she said in a beautiful Spanish accent.

"Wait, no, that's alright. We can just talk for second."

"Fuck me."

"It's ok. Hold on. I just wanted to talk to you. That's all. I think you're a beautiful person, and maybe we can get out of control sometimes—out of place, you know? But things can get better, better than they seem anyway..."

The prostitute was confused. I couldn't tell if it was due to the fact that she didn't understand English or if it was due to the fact that I wasn't having sex with her. Regardless, the affects of the oxycontin was making me feel extremely warm and hypersensitive.

"There is happiness to be found," I continued. "Look, everywhere. There are sunsets, fields of tulips, kindness and love; we take it for granted, and we don't see our inner-self, so beautiful and happy. I see people with sad faces all the time; it's an illusion they can't get past."

She grew intolerant to my words. She looked at her watch, then began to dress.

"Wait. Where are you going," I pleaded. "Don't go. It's ok."

"HECTOR!" she yelled.

"Wait. I'm sorry. I didn't mean to hurt you."

"HECTOR!"

She made her way to the door. Outside I heard a voice. The door opened and a shadowy figure grabbed her by the arm and pulled her out. The door quickly shut behind her.

Suddenly my stomach felt ill and I broke out in a cold sweat. I hunched over and puked on the carpet. Everything inside my body was being forced out, my guts, my blood, my soul. It was loud and deathly, and I couldn't stop. There were four or five dry-heaves before I managed to my feet. I tried to gain focus. My teary eyes had become sensitive to the light, everything was blurred. I opened the door to a liquid figure standing in the hallway. I kept my hands on the wall, guiding myself through, to the end of the hallway, past the man at the desk. I heard the sounds of distorted, diabolical laughter echoing from behind. I found the door and hurried to escape. As I opened the door, a rush of cool air went up through my nose. I now had a second wind, brought graciously by the Gods. At that moment, I knew I had to do the most important thing in my life: get back to LA and sign up for rehab.

I got back to the hotel with the clock reading 3:42 and Big Curls face down in bed. I checked his vital signs and realized he was just sleeping. I sat on the bed and only managed my shoes off before laying my head down. I stared at the ceiling and peacefully asked the spirits for a second chance. The border patrol agents, the k-9s, guns, searchlights and sirens—they'd all be there, patiently waiting. I prayed for a safe trip home, just one more opportunity to go straight. My eyes began to melt, the blackness came, and like a sharp cape across me eyes, I fell asleep.

CRAWL FETCH SPOON

BY

REINA NIECE

Crawl Fetch Spoon

She awakes.

The same as before. How much?

I have to consider Kyle. I have to. What's he going to do? These repetitive questions run through my blood, over and over—shit lasting, spinning my mind. I can't help it. I try tuning it out. I suddenly escape to a lost thought, years ago when my younger brother was taken to the hospital. He was 6-years-old with a 105 degree temperature. The whole time he cried, the tears only cooling the surface of his cheeks. He had a confused look on his face. He couldn't understand where the pain was coming from. There was nothing external, no one touching him, or teasing him, or pinching the back of his arm. The pain was coming from within. And it wasn't his pain that made me cringe, it was his confusion, his innocent look, the *why* and *how* in his eyes. He went on blaming everything: the nurse, the blanket, mom, me, the lights, the bed. We were all to blame. There was nothing for him, no outlet for his pain. I suddenly realize that this is me now. I can only blame everything. And my fever is fake, nothing like his. But either way, I blame. Either way, it still hurts.

I worry these days. I worry about the disease they said on tv. I'm sure it's in me. The disease, I can feel it. It sometimes feels like I'm going to collapse. It comes over me like a wave, like the great hawk that smoothers you in your dreams. In my mind I know it's wrong.

I call Kyle.

"Where are you?"

"I'm at the park."

I don't say anything. I wait for him to give me the news.

"I'm waiting for Henry."

"What's he got?"

"I don't know. I have to go."

I hang up without saying goodbye.

I used to love him. But the flower's sap has drained out of me, to this drowning face I see in the mirror, white, scabbing, gums bleeding. In my mind I know it's wrong. I keep staring at the watermarked mirror and Kyle's old, job-hunting stubbles stuck to a soap-scum sink. I don't want the water to run on me. I stay away.

I sit on the floor and wrap my arms around my legs. I rock back and forth. The cold, it comes again. My withered arms do their best to hold on tight. I close my eyes. Every ounce of energy used and trying ... keep it out!—this fucking light!

Now Kyle!

Now!

I don't want to have to call you again. I need to know. And don't play these fucking games! I'm gonna take what's left. I don't care if you beat me again. I don't care anymore.

Sip. Push. Recycled blood spinning like a red cloud through a liquid sky. I feel better, yet apart of me feels I wasted it. I should have taken it sooner, before the muffin in my stomach. I could have felt it more. That fucking muffin took it away. Shit, no. Please!

Of course he enters with a smile. Of course that fucking smile, that smile I'd like to punch. Little beady eyes I'd like to gouge out of his skull. But I know he has it. Kyle never entered with a smile unless he had it.

"Did you get any?"

He doesn't say anything, just hurriedly sits on the couch and takes the shit out of the brown paper bag. I sit next to him. Suddenly I love him again. I feel loyal to him. He's my dear, my man. It's hard to see, but it's more than I thought. I see the flame. He brings it to my arm. I am warm again.

The phone rings. I let it ring. Apart of me wants to answer it. I am happy and I want to share my happiness. Those calling asking for help, poor people. I move towards the phone, though it has stopped ringing some time ago. I pick it up and hear a dial tone.

I reach for Kyle. He's passed out on the couch. I smell the layers of sweat on his back, layers and layers, like wax—over weeks, clogging pores. And the bugs do their best to feed on his skin. There are holes in his face, his hair greasy and dying. He is lost like me. He is thin like me. He is absorbed like me. The drug never appreciates a traitor. You're either in or you're out. I don't have the energy to fight it. The drive and discipline left me a long time ago.

"Wake up, Kyle!" I urge. "Wake up!"

"*What?*"

"I just wana know ... alive?"

"I'm here," he says. "I'm here."

We surf the waves of black waters. The distant moon casting a silver lining across the crest of our shallow waves. We strive to reach it, spin away, only hoping to come back again. We take it for granted, and if we can't make it, we drown in questions that never seem to stop...

This mind has become a disposable wasteland for only one thing: a wasteland that doesn't accept plastic or cardboard, organics, or tin. It will only consider the Few. Turning things down never mattered, things only get in the way. This time we spend sulking, lifting, turning and praying. This is the time we watch ourselves taken by the tide.

"Kyle! Wake up!"

I lie there next to him.

I fall asleep dreaming of clowns dancing in fire.

✷ ✷ ✷

Myla is my love. A shih tzu, 2 years old. She sleeps by my leg. She protects me against strangers. I look at her. She is so beautiful. Her black lips and round eyes. What have I done, Myla? Look at this place, will ya? I need to feed you, I know.

I look at the stacks of mail, mostly credit card burden. But then a letter or two from Alan De Silva. His correspondence is eloquent as he describes the downfalls. And I can't blame him for wanting out. He only did it to experience life, to write about it. Now he's stuck. He writes:

This blur, my dear ... is that force that takes us away from the scope of reason. Yet to please the virgin senses is a crusade I must go. I can only spill so much blood before the water hounds take their stance against me. They'll find me as now my wind battered ship can only sail the all-knowing current...

I try to write back to him, but the sound of the typer bothers my nerves. Click, smack! ... click, smack! click, smack! ... *ZIPPPP!* Click, pull, crumble: painful vibrations of sound and black ink on stale white, like a tattoo on virgin skin. I want silence, but the silence scares me. So I pace back and forth in the room, thinking, walking, thinking, turning, here again, turn, bleed. Kyle still dead on the couch. I stare at him and realize I want to move back. Florida's sun never murdered so many. I picture myself back in Jersey, my parents, my brother back from India, and me drinking water, purging this sickness away for good. Oh, my mom. She loves me so much and I love her. We fight, I know, but I love her. She is so beautiful, those photos from when she was younger. Her face made the poor film look so bright and beautiful. I want to talk to her and tell her I love her and that I miss her and I want to come home. And I know I'm hurting your feelings, mom. I know I'm married and I know you want grandchildren. More than anything you want grandchildren. But I want to come home again. I'm so sorry, but I can't do this anymore.

I put my face in front of the fan. It blows my sticky sweat cool, running my hair behind my shoulders. Suddenly I want to be touched again. The gods above me, I can feel them. They circle with grace and love. Myla comes to me and licks my leg. I pick her up and hold her close. I sit next to Kyle and run my hand through his hair one last time. I can't blame him anymore. He is a beautiful person too. I wish it had worked out, Kyle, I really do, but I have wasted too much time drowning in a flame that will only burn if I don't let you go.

I pick up the phone, the dial tone is loud. I slowly dial the numbers: 973...

"Mom?"

"Oh, hey, sweetie! How are you?"

"I have to say something, and don't want you to be upset," I say on the verge of tears.

"What's the matter? Is everything ok?"

I can't hold back the tears. Everything I had done wrong in the last 3 years finally spills. Accepting sickness. A wave of sorrow pulls everything out. I'm graciously left stripped, void of feelings, hollowed to start anew. This is my blessing as my guilt no longer controls me.

"I'm sorry, mom. I really am. I have to come home."

"What happened?"

"I'm on drugs."

✵ ✵ ✵

I wait at a hotel. 16 missed calls, 9 from Kyle, every phantom trying to bring me back. They sense it; they somehow know I'm leaving. Bastards of the underground won't accept being alone, they know—all too true, they know. But I'm disciplined now. I'm firm, focused—only one direction, only one place to go. Mom, please. Where are you? Until you're here I won't feel safe. Mother please, I can't sit still. Where is my aggression? Merciless life is the only way. I must question reason and appeal to logic. Never mind. Nobody truly feels sorry for anyone. Yeah, you might get a tear from mom, and if you're lucky, a little sympathy from father—but no one cares, no one gives a shit. Trapped, webbed in responsibility, caught like a wingless maggot feeding on its own legs. Whether we like it or not, suckers could never shoot enough, never get enough, never accept being alone in their own little worthless presence. It will all eventually catch up to you.

There is a knock at the door. My mother comes in with a great big hug. I see my father's sunkin face over her shoulder. He's worried sick. It appears he's lost wait. Oh, my Italian father with swollen eyes and rosy cheeks, you always wanted what's best for me. I can't find the words to say how sorry I am; I just cry now. I just cry. And it feels like I haven't seen them in a decade. They look different, they look old and stressed, sick. What have they done since I've been gone? I miss them. Their old, patient skin touching mine.

I make it back to NJ. Morristown. In a glowing house cradled against the snow. I was born here, raised here. New Jersey, my home. I'm proud to say I'm from here. I miss everything about it, little things that I never thought I would. There's a special gravity here, a gravity that instantly captured me when I got off the plane.

I walk the Morristown green and think about my past, wanting to let it all go. I pass some of the shops noticing new lights, new colors, and feeling new vibes. The place is different. I pick up the local magazine. Now there's an art movement. Painters and writers, poets and musicians. They've sprung up from nowhere. Some of the work is amazing. It's a pleasant distraction, an outlet for trapped feelings, a healing process for those who feel distant to the common way of life. I realize I need this. Much like my sickened x, much like my sickened brother, I too need an outlet to release the pain.

I find an article on Alan. He's doing a reading at The Coffee Shop in Madison next Tuesday. I can't wait to see him. He's one of the few that can understand. I decide to write a story, this story, and give it to him.

I type the last words and look at my dear Myla.

"It's finished, precious. Let's take a walk."

☆ ☆ ☆

PONYTAIL

Ponytail

I decided to take the train to New York City. I had been to the Village a few times, read a few stories from *The Lost Scripts of the Underground*. With these beautiful women in sleek leather fashions, black zip-ups, long hair, pierced eyes and lips. They were like sharp needles scratching along a soft harmony, forcing that violent rhythm against the mundane. And I'd watch them move, blood-poisoned tattoos marching fast, poised like blades. By the sound of their boots you could almost say they owned the streets. Approaching these women was talent, an eccentric vibe, artistic vision. Ignore. Spit certain mockeries. Twist the story. Most importantly, remain focused. The second they sense weakness is the second they turn.

I entered a bar on Bleeker St. An Asian bartender serving drinks with embellished smiles of gratitude. Oh, she was so proud—joyful in her new position as bartender. Now she was apart of it, an intricate force behind a great city function.

I sat at the bar and ordered a drink, something with fragile sugar, something to lift the blood.

"Vodka-7, please."

"Sure!" she said with a rubber smile. She raced to the other side of the bar, quickly grabbed the vodka and swooped a glass through the ice. She poured a 7-count. I watched the bubbles race up, shooting stars in a clear glass. She placed a napkin and looked at me with lust-driven eyes.

"You like a menu?"

"No thanks."

"Ok," she said softly, "if you need anything else let me know."

She sat the drink down and slowly slid her hand down the glass. Perhaps it was easier than I thought. Perhaps I lucked out. Just work a little game at the bar. I reminded myself that I had been in this position several times. Bartenders had tendencies to rub sex in your face for an extra tip.

She walked to the other side of the bar where a girl was sitting. It seemed as though the other girl was also an employee. She sat there drinking water, talking intermittently with the bartender. I noticed the bartender whispering to the girl. A loud burst of laughter came as they looked at me. The bartender grabbed a remote off the bar and started changing radio stations.

"What kind of music do you like?" she asked.

"Do you have any Oingo Boingo?"

"What?"

"Oingo Boingo. It's an 80's band."

"Oh, you like 80's! Oh, me too!" she said, switching the satellite radio to 80's music. Men at Work, *It's a Mistake*, hit the air. She sat the remote down and walked over.

"So what's your name?"

"Jamison."

"My name is Miwa."

"Miwa? Where are you from?"

"Well, I was born in Bolivia, but I'm half Japanese............
M E !!! ... I ... ... O H ... ... !!! ... ... I ... ... O H ...
M E ... ... !!! ... ... M E ... !!! ... ... M E ... ... O H ... ... !!!
... ... I ... !!! ... ... !!! ... I ... O H ... !!! ... ... M E ... ... !!! ... ...
I ... .!!! ... ..."

A long, speed-med story about her parents and how they settled in South America. Her story continued like a dead man dragged by horse across the Sahara. I soon realized that she wasn't the most popular girl. She was annoying. Her voice went into tail-spins as she shifted along various stories about her life. She had been in NYC for only a year, and from the sound of it, she was having problems fitting in. She loved NYC, said it was the best place she'd ever been. But it was so hard to make a living, she worked two jobs, never got any free time, no friends. Looking close, I suddenly realized the whites of her eyes were deep purple, shot from trying to stay up with the City. Even so, she still had loads of energy, and a static spunk that would turn most people away.

"That's interesting," I said. "I haven't met too many people from South America."

"I plan on going back for the holidays."

"To see your parents?"

"Yes, and my dog Kika! *Oh*, I miss her so much!"

I thought of asking about her dog, but I knew it would just lead to another long story. Instead, I took a sip and headed towards the bathroom. I noticed on the bathroom stall: *FOR AN ELIZABETH HAND HAND JOB CALL 1-800-LIZ-HAND.* I was in a piss-drained stupor staring at the advertisement when suddenly I devised a plan to leave.

I came back to the bar.

"Can I check out, please?"

"Leaving me so soon?"

"Yeah, I'm sorry. I have to meet up with some friends."

"Where are you guys going?"

"I don't know yet. I have to call them."

She came back with the check. She stared at me as though waiting for something. She kept staring, looking at me with anticipating eyes. She leaned over the bar. I could see the top half of her breasts. They were fairly small, but appeared solid, perfectly round. I pretended not to notice. I looked at the check. She had comped me a drink. I began doing the math in my head. The comped drink. Sex on the glass. There was no pen. I looked up, hoping she'd realize that I couldn't sign off.

"Hey thanks," I said. "Do you happen to have a pen?"

"Oh, now you want something from me," she said in a teasing tone. She took a pen out of her back pocket. She held the pen over the bar. I reached to grab it. She took it back, slid the check her way, and wrote her number down.

"Call me in hour. I have someone covering for me at 10. I know of a party."

"Sure. I'll let you know."

I grabbed my cell phone and pretended to store her number in my phone. I tipped her 30%, plus the comp.

✩ ✩ ✩

I walked out to the street. Humid air blurring an orange moon. I walked a few blocks down to 9th. I saw a bar with people dancing, dressed in costume. I approached the bouncer. He had greasy hair and aggravated eyes, his fat neck folded in tubes of fat.

"What's the cover to get in?" I asked.

"It's a private party," he said, looking the other way.

I headed down the street to an adjacent alleyway. Lit up a cigarette. Across the way a black cat peeped its head out from a nook in the brick wall. It looked at me with glowing green eyes. Suddenly a door kicked opened. The cat ran into the street dodging cars. Two Latino kids sliding out trash cans filled with empty beer bottles. A wave of sound coming from within. The party. The music. I caught the door just before it closed. One of the Latino kids saw me, but he was too far away to catch me. I walked in like I knew the place, through the kitchen, into the masquerade. A DJ spinning beats, laser lights, women dancing, holding close—some kissing, grinding hips. I ordered a shot from the bar. Hit it. One more. Hit it. Then on the dance floor dancing. Terrible dancer finding new rhythm. Internalizing the beat, moving like a cartoon of happiness, feeding on collective ecstasy. Then against a warm body, the contouring firm. Solid. Round. Hard. Motions between us, pulsating base. I grabbed her hips, pulled her close, her fissure felt through tight black pants. I wanted more. I wanted to grab her neck, her hair. I knew it would cross the line. We danced hard, like we had nothing else to give. Across the room was a mirror. I noticed myself dancing. I was moving awkward, stiff, trying to keep up.

I decided to take a break. I walked back to the bar and noticed another guy had quickly moved in. He was behind her sliding up and down. She bent over, keeping her back arched. She glanced back at him. Her eyes spoke of electricity, of deep vibrations. Veins protruded up her neck. She wanted to feel the burst—hours upon hours, built energy shot all at once. She continued with the rhythm, running her fingers through her hair, raising, pulling tight. She held her hair back as she rubbed against him. They continued dancing through the smoke, like dark angels enjoying a brief moment in the clouds.

I looked across the room, the DJ in a small box above the dance floor. She spun the beats under a dim light. I thought about her job and was suddenly inspired. I wanted to give up everything and become a DJ. This DJ, doctor of social tensions, therapeutic beats, like an artistic night-life humanitarian—spinning music, forcing the release of trapped feelings naked on the floor. I knew nothing about spinning; but at that moment, I was cast in delusion and had no doubts that I could do it better than anyone in the world.

I ordered a beer. Then a sharp and angry finger poked me in the back. I instantly thought I was caught, the security guard from outside was tipped off. Of course, I had no costume. I looked behind me and there stood Miwa, the top half of her face covered in a mask of feathers. She wore a short black skirt and black boots that went up to her knees.

"You were supposed to call me!" she yelled over the music.

"I'm sorry. I was actually about to."

"Yeah, right!"

She grabbed me by the arm and pulled me across the dance floor. We made our way towards the other side, towards the entrance door. I stopped before we got too close.

"Hey, wait." I said. "Where are we going?"

"I want to have a cigarette outside, so we can talk."

I was too embarrassed to tell her I had came through the back, so I followed her out hoping I could somehow get back in. I turned my head as we passed the security guard. We stood on the sidewalk next to a subway grate. The faint smell of rat piss rose up in a steam. She waited with a cigarette in her mouth.

"So, is this the party you knew of?" I said, lighting her cigarette.

"I'm mad at you."

"Why? I was gonna call."

"You must be a layer."

"A what?"

"You! A layer!"

"A layer? What's a layer... oh, you must mean a player."

"A player, yes! So, tell me. Are you a player?"

"No, not really."

"*Auh*, not really. So you're not saying you're not."

"Actually, I've never been with a girl."

"HA, HA, HA, HA, HA, HA, HA, HA!! You funny!!"

Her ear-shattering laughter furthered her annoyance to the world.

"So," she continued, "you want to dance with me?"

"I have to forewarn you, I'm not a good dancer."

"Fooowie! Every player is a good dancer. Come on."

Again she grabbed my arm and pulled me behind her. I was beginning to feel like I was her pet. We approached the door and the bouncer immediately recognized me. He stopped us before entering.

"I can't let you in," he said.

"He's with me," Miwa responded.

"I'm sorry. He's not on the list."

"That's ok," I said to Miwa, hoping she'd go in without me. "I'll call you later."

"Wait. I'll talk to him. Give me one second."

She leaned towards the bouncer and whispered something in his ear. The bouncer smiled but shook his head. She whispered something more.

The bouncer turned away. Miwa kept talking, trying to convince him. Her voice became increasingly louder.

"What is the matter with you! You're no good!"

I came in, grabbed her on the shoulder. "It's ok," I said. "I can just go and we can meet up some other time."

She pulled away, her face screaming veins of anger at the bouncer.

"I can't believe you! I know your name! I know you! You just wait, Mr. Big Man! Mr. Big man with big belly!" She stormed away, turning her back and pompously flipping her air. She forced her arm around mine and brought us to the edge of the sidewalk. "Let's get out of here," she said, flagging a cab.

I didn't want to upset her. I knew leaving was not an option. I looked at her and noticed she was breathing heavy through her nose; her nostrils flaring out with each rapid intake. She hailed a cab, not saying a word.

After giving the driver the address she remained silent. Occasional I'd look at her. She was in some type of zone. It was as if no one else existed. She was intently focused on her anger, channeling it ... below, somewhere. I suddenly liked her. She was the loyal type, she would die for the one she loved. I rolled down the window. The sudden air whipping through, blowing her feathers and hair across her face. She lifted her mask and looked at me. She smiled, then looked away.

The cab driver accelerated, jolting the wheel as he weaved through slowing cars. The bright lights blurring; the cool wind through our hair. It felt like we were traveling through time; it made me feel safe, even though the driving was extremely reckless.

We arrived outside her apartment. Upper-west side. She was hesitant to invite me in. Outside her door, waiting. Then the motion elevating to a maybe. I don't know. Indecisive seconds. Ok. Come in. I followed her past the security guard, a big black man who gave me a smile suggesting I was in for a ride. To the elevator. Chime. We're here. Inside her apartment. 14th floor. Small place, twin size bed against the only window. Dishware, towels, clothes, even a mountain bike supported on hook-screws.

She took off her jacket and went to bathroom. I sat on the couch and thought about the train schedule. I had missed the train before and was stranded in the city for a night. One of the many littered pitfalls living in Jersey. Miwa came out and sat next to me on the couch.

"So, you like my place?"

"Yeah, it's real nice."

"It's a little small, but I'm looking to move pretty soon."

"Where to?"

"I don't know yet. Maybe the Village. I would be closer to work."

"This is true."

"So," she said, putting her hand on my leg, "what do you do?"

"Nothing."

"Nothing? Well, you have to do something."

"I don't."

"Well, then how do you eat?"

"I put it on the credit card."

"Come on. Tell me."

I pulled out my wallet and gave her a business card. She read the words: *"Jamison Loft. A Fiction Writer Who Has Never Been Paid For His Fiction Writing."*

"You're a writer!" she exclaimed.

"Not officially."

"Oh, but I'm sure you're good!"

"How do you know?"

"I can see it in your eyes. You just have that look, like you know something secret."

"I don't have any secrets, just words that never seem to stop."

"I'm gonna be your number one fan."

"Sure. I have to start somewhere."

"Perfect! Let's celebrate!"

She made her way to the fridge. Her tight black skirt, the knee high boots—a simple equation that could turn any man on. Her body was firm, contoured. She had sway-back posture, a thin waist. She returned with two beers. I popped them open with my lighter. We tapped glasses and said cheers to 80's music.

"So how's the view," I asked.

"It's nice."

"I guess I have to get on your bed to check it out?"

"Are you scared of my bed?"

"No."

"You should be."

"Why's that?"

She looked down as though embarrassed.

"I'm a little crazy."

I got up, made my way to the bed. I crawled on my knees to the window. I pulled the draw string. Outside, the lights of the city, the blood line of cars running through the streets. I turned around and noticed Miwa standing next to the bed, wearing only her boots and a black thong.

"Which view do you like better?" she asked.

I involuntarily let go of the draw string. The blinds slammed shut. I slowly approached her. Just before I came off the bed, she met me with a stiff arm, pushing back on. She threw me down and immediately straddled me. Grabbing my wrists, she forced my arms above my head. She teased with her nose close to mine.

"What's your favorite color?" she asked.

"Well, that depends on the season," I said, lifting up trying to kiss her. She backed away as though I was venomous to her needs.

"Tell me," she pleaded in a passionate whisper.

"I can't give out that information."

Her eyes quickly shifted to her bed post.

"I have green, yellow, blue, red … *black*."

"How bout orange?" I said, looking across my shoulder noticing an assortment of hair ties around the bed post. There must have been close to 100 of them.

"I may have that, if you're lucky."

She swung her leg over my body, exposing her ass close to my face. I had this instant desire to grab her. I was teething at the thought. I put my hand on her ass; it was cold and hard. She arched her back which made her ass seem bigger, more round. It begged for needle-prick pain. She kept searching for the orange, taking her time as I massaged her ass, loosing the muscles, making it warm. She put an orange hair tie around her wrist, then came over and straddled me again.

"You like orange?"

"Yes, I do," I said, noticing my voice had gone soft and frail.

She took the orange hair tie and pulled her hair back into a ponytail.

"I hate it when my hair gets in the way."

She loosened my belt and pulled my pants down. In the process, my underwear partially came off. She pulled them back up, as though savoring the moment. She untied my shoes and took my pants off. She came up and spent minutes breathing close and heavy on the spot. Her hot breath making it warm. I felt the moisture build beneath. She struggled pulling it out. I was bulging face down; the underwear stretched around me. She tracked it with her hand, from the top, all the way down, her nails scratching my legs as she went. She found the bottom and flipped it up. She pulled my underwear over the top.

I felt the cool air running across the sweat. She blew on it, cool air. I retracted up, stiff and hard. She went down to the bottom and licked all the way up. She came up, standing straight on her knees. She looked into my eyes.

"I'm gonna try to take it. When I'm almost there I want you to smack me."

She turned around on all fours, her ass again next to my face. I put my hand on her ass as she went down. She didn't waste any time. I was half hard, just enough for her to stretch it with her mouth. Latching with her teeth, pulling it, stretching it. It hurt, but I was into it. Soon I was rock hard. I looked down and didn't recognize myself. I was bigger than usual. She turned around, still holding me upright.

"You ready?" she asked.

I nodded.

She put it in her mouth. Almost there before she choked. I smacked her. She came up. A few strokes on top, twisting her mouth. Then back down. A pause. The extra effort to take it all in. I smacked her. This time a little harder. I felt myself break through the barrier. I was in her throat. She came up gasping for air, strings of saliva still connected to her mouth. She looked at me with eyes tearing. She turned around, her ponytail in the air. She took it again. Trying desperately, punishing herself with her repressed envy. She grabbed my hand and put it on her ponytail. I gripped her hair tight, pulling her facial skin to new youth. She tried once more, almost there. She grabbed my hand and made me release her ponytail. She held my hand flat like hers and forced me to hit her on the back of the head. It felt weird. I didn't want to hurt her. Still, she insisted. Hit me! Punch me! I want it! I lightly tapped her on the back of the head. She shook her head no. Harder! I couldn't force myself to do it. She increased her speed, up and down, faster, the bed bouncing up and down. I felt it building, it was coming. At the right moment she hit herself on the back of the head. I grabbed her by the ponytail and pulled her off. She pleaded no. Don't cum! I exploded. The first shot across the room. She squeezed and put her other hand over the top. Don't cum! She was forcing it to stop. She squeezed hard, clogging. Nothing more was coming out. I suddenly felt an immense amount of pain.

"Auh, shit!"

"Please! No!"

I forced her hands away and tried to continue, but it had stopped inside me. It felt like I had strained every internal muscle possible, like someone had shot me in the lower gut. I was in crimpled pain, trying to find my clothes. I wanted out of there. She kept grabbing my arm, pleading me not to go. I told her I was going to miss the train, had to leave. As I dressed she began to masturbate.

"Does this turn you on?"

"It does, but I have to go. I'll call you."

I left out the front door, down the elevator. I walked passed the security guard holding my stomach. He took one look, laughing hysterically—that deep, diabolical laughter echoing through the hall. I came out the front door and puked in large planter next to the entrance. I hailed a cab. Train station. Please hurry. I caught the last train just in time. Back to Morristown. I looked at my phone, a text message from Aubrey. *What's up stranger?* Aubrey was innocent, religious girl from Drew University. English major, straight and narrow. At that moment I desperately wanted to ask her out. Maybe next weekend we could do something simple, like candle light, movie by the fire. Just the thought of kissing her was enough. That's all I wanted, take it slow, nothing too serious. I closed my eyes and pictured her calming smile.

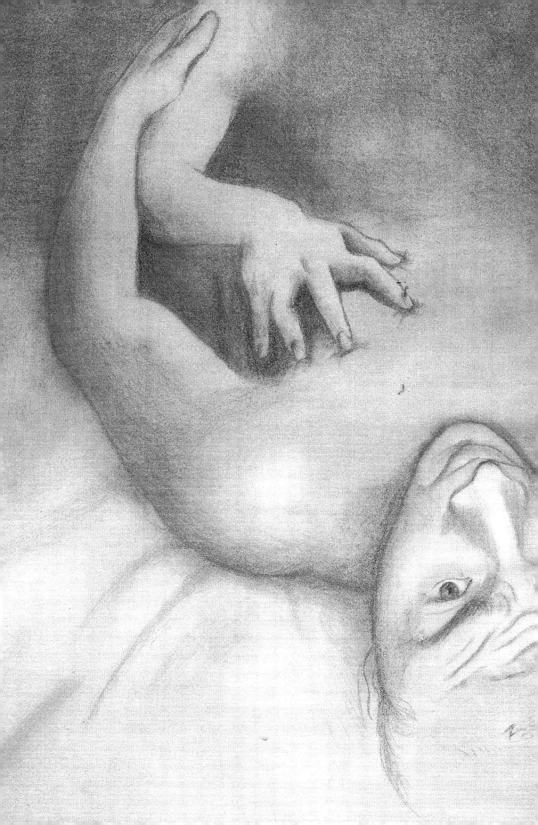

GOOD-BYE TO YOU CELIBATE SUN

1981.

The pain in my lower abdomen was getting worse.

It would often come at night when I'd least expect it. I wasn't sure how to react as the thought of telling my father made me feel ashamed. I didn't know why I felt this way, I just did. So I went on feeling helpless, nursing a weakness that continued to plague me alone.

My room was mostly dark. I could barely see the shadows of my dresser and closet. Across the floor were tiny yellow beads of light that had seeped through the blinds from a street light outside my window. Like a necklace of neon pearls, the beads were strung linear by a thin stream of light. I stared at the beads and thought about Mrs. Carpenito's lecture on constellations. She told us about the stars, how they make patterns in the night sky. The stars, she said at the end, are like a billion souls punctured through a great black sheet.

Soon I heard the sound of a distant car. As it neared, the radiant beads began to swell. Each one intensified, glowing brighter as they slowly moved up the wall. The car quickly passed causing the beads to suddenly merge to a wavy pool of aqua light on the ceiling. The light danced only for a moment. Then the sound of the car faded, the ceiling light disappeared; and the beads, once again, aligned linear on the floor.

It was during one of these celestial moments that I heard for the first time the stifled moans from the other room. It started out as murmured panting, but gradually intensified into something heavy and vicious. I could feel the brooding strength coming undone; the desperate, uncontrolled sounds quickly rising to a submissive scream. Suddenly I found myself in a new state; I felt insecure with my body and mind. I didn't understand. I just knew that somehow these sounds triggered an emotion dormant within. From that moment, for whatever reason, I knew I never wanted to hurt anyone.

The morning came and I quickly dressed in my pajamas. I ran to the tv knowing Batman and Robin would be on channel 3. The Joker had a new trap this time: a large tub of slimy green acid awaited the tied up and suspended Batman and Robin. The Joker was slowly luring them closer.

"What are you watching?" my father asked.

"Batman and Robin."

"Yeah, who's winning?"

"Look! The Joker is going to kill them!"

My father sat next to me on the floor.

"I bet you Batman and Robin find a way to escape," my father said.

"But look! They're getting closer!"

Our anticipation was halted by a commercial.

"Dad?"

"Yeah, bud?"

"Where's mom?"

There was a slight pause before he spoke. I knew there was something wrong. My father searched for the right words: "Well, she's away for now. But she will visit sometimes, and she's always thinking about you."

Batman and Robin returned and instantly my attention fled to the screen. "Here it is! Shhhh!" The dynamic duo, with hands bound, awaiting their fate below: *"You'll never get away with it, Joker,"* Robin proclaimed. *"Only fools would think such a thing,"* Joker responded. *"Your days are numbered, and with you two out of the picture, I will be on my way to take over Gotham City."* Batman forced one of his hands loose just in time to escape and free Robin. A fight ensued, and the Joker forged his escape through a back door. Batman and Robin were once again victorious.

I jumped up in excitement, my father catching me in mid-air, quickly swinging me back to my feet. He held up his hand for a high-five. "See, I told you they'd get out of it."

I sat back on the floor anxious for the next episode.

"Hello, Jamison," a lady's soft voice said from behind me.

There in the hallway stood Jody, my babysitter from when I was a few years younger. Recently I had seen her a few times, here and there. She wore a faded red robe, loosely fitted; her makeup was slightly smeared across her skin. Her face was chubby and always seemed to have an overly concerned look to it. There was something about Jody I didn't like. It seemed as if she ascribed to a certain formula when communicating with me. She always used the same words, just different sometimes. "Hi, Jamison. How are you?"

"Hi," I said.

"You remember Jody, don't you?" my father asked.

"Yeah, she was my babysitter."

"That's right. And remember when you cracked your head open and she took care of you?"

"Yeah."

I had accidentally run into a glass door at Jody's house. My head was split open and I was taken to the hospital for fourteen stitches. Jody made sure I was taken care of before my mother picked me up.

"I don't need a babysitter anymore," I bitterly announced.

My father and Jody looked at each other.

"She's just here to make sure everything is ok," my father said. "That's all."

The phone rang.

"I'll get it!" I said.

I ran over, picked up. It was my mother.

"Hi, honey. How are you?"

"Fine."

"Whatcha doin?"

"Watchin tv with dad and Jody."

"Jody? Babysitter Jody?"

"Yep."

"Oh … well that's nice. So how's school?"

"Fine."

"Yeah, how's your teacher this year."

"Fine. She's teaching us how to make Christmas cards."

"*Oh, wow!*"

"Hey, mom?"

"Yeah, sweetie?"

"Are you going to be here for Christmas?"

"I will definitely see you for Christmas. You don't have to worry about that. In fact, I'm coming over in a couple hours to pick you up."

"You are!"

"I'll be there soon, ok."

"Ok."

"Ok, so let me talk to your father."

I gave the phone to my father and ran back to the tv. A new episode started, except this time it was the Penguin forcing his diabolic will on the crypt crusaders. Suddenly from the other room I could hear my father's voice.

"There is nothing going on ... He doesn't know! ... Look, I'm not going to argue with you! ... She's just over because she wanted to see him! ... It's not like that! ... Of course he's innocent! ... Fine, see you then!"

My father slammed the phone down. His face turned bright red. Jody quickly went to his side. "See this is what I'm talking about," my father said. "She just doesn't seem to get it." Jody began coaxing him, rubbing his back with a soft hand. She looked at him with sagging, raccoon eyes. Soon his breathing slowed, his face turned to a light blush. "She's going to be here soon. It would probably be best if you left for awhile."

"Ok," Jody said. "I'll be at the house if you need me."

Jody left and my father went back to his bedroom.

I continued watching Batman.

It wasn't long before the door bell rang and my mother entered. I ran into her arms—that lost scent of lavender surrounded me, her soft check against mine.

"It's so good to see you," she said, rocking me back and forth in her arms. "How about we get some ice cream on our way back?"

"Yeah!"

My father entered the room.

"So, you'll have him back on Monday?" he asked.

My mother looked up and saw my father standing with his arms crossed. She tapped me on the shoulder. "Go ahead and wait for me in the car, honey." I grabbed my small duffle bag along with my Tonka truck and headed outside. Immediately, I noticed something wrong. Her car wasn't the same. Instead of her green Volvo Station Wagon, she now drove a decrepit Pontiac Ventura. Something deeply bothered me about this. I wanted her old car back. The Pontiac looked too masculine—the silver color, the shape of a dying sports car. The whole thing just didn't seem right for her.

She came out the front door with a dismal look on her face. I looked up at her and the second we made eye contact her expression changed. She smiled and said: "So what kind of ice cream do you want?"

"Vanilla."

"That's it? Just plain ol' vanilla?"

"Yep."

"Well that's no fun."

After ice cream we took a ride to my mother's new place. We walked into the front room. I noticed a bunch of boxes filled with my mother's old possessions, including her childhood Raggedy Anne doll from when she was younger.

Talking on the phone in the kitchen was a freckled, pale-faced man. He had a receding hairline, exposing small red blotches on his flaky scalp.

"I'm still in the process of settling in," my mother said. "Come here. I want you to meet someone." We made our way to the kitchen. The man noticed us and quickly hung up the phone to greet us.

"Hey!" he said, as though we were long lost pals. "You must be Jamison!"

"Jamie," my mother said, "I want you to meet Mark. Mark has been helping me move these last couple of weeks."

"Hi."

"He's a little shy right now," she said to Mark. "So did you get a tee time?"

"Yeah, 3:15 with JR."

"Great. Samantha is coming to pick me up at 1:30 to do some shopping. Perhaps you and Jamison can get to know each other out on the course."

"Why, sure! Jamison, have you ever seen a golf course before?"

"No."

"That's great. You'll get to see one for the first time today."

I didn't respond. I was upset over the fact that I had been set up. I really wanted to spend time with my mother, but now I felt betrayed. She had previously planned this with Mark. Now I was going to be away from her, and with someone I didn't even know.

Samantha arrived and my mother kissed me on the cheek good-bye. Mark didn't say much once they left. He occupied most his time on the phone, speaking with different people about motorcycles, engine parts, Dallas Cowboy Cheerleaders, and guns. After a while he approached me, lit up a cigarette and said: "Well, kid, you ready?" His voice was different from before. It seemed more direct and serious, less sophisticated in tone. At the schoolyard calling someone "kid" was a tactic for degrading another classmate. Fights were often fueled by this word choice. I instantly got the feeling he saw less in me than I had originally thought.

We got into the Pontiac and drove off. Inside the driver side door was a Budweiser sticker that I hadn't noticed before. It dawned on me that the car might actually be Mark's.

"Is this your car?" I asked.

"It most certainly is."

"What happened to my mom's car?"

"She sold it."

"Why?"

"She needed the money."

"Why?"

"Hey, kid, moving is expensive."

We arrived at the golf course early. Mark set the ignition so we could still here the radio. The Doobie Brother's, "Black Water," played on. Mark began singing the chorus while changing his shoes.

"So, you'll have to wait here for a little bit," he said. "I've got to meet up with JR and then I'll get you when we're ready. I'll leave the radio on." Mark popped the trunk and retrieved his golf clubs, then walked towards the club-house.

It seemed like I was in the car for hours. The heat eventually built up. Even with the windows down, I felt hot and began to sweat. Periodically, I would leave the car to walk around and cool off. Occasionally I'd hear a song I liked and force myself back into the car. I started to play a game with myself to see whether I could predict the next song. I kept score. As it turned out I was wrong on every occasion. It was Steve Miller's, "Fly Like an Eagle," when Mark finally got back.

"So, kid, you ready to play some golf?"

"I don't know how."

"Well, you can watch and learn."

I noticed his eyes were blood-shot, his shirt partially twisted around his waist. He now walked around with a jagged saunter. Behind the car was the golf cart, his golf bag strapped in the back, a beer and coke in the beverage holders.

"Can I drive it?" I asked.

"Not now. We'll have to wait until we get on the course. Come on, I got you a coke."

We drove up in the cart to the starting booth. A well dressed man in polo took a ticket from Mark and directed us to the first tee. JR was already there practicing his swing. Mark took a long swig from his beer before grabbing his driver and approaching JR on the elevated tee.

"Alright," Mark adamantly proclaimed. "For each hole there will be a five dollar bet per stroke."

"Five dollars?" JR responded. "That seems a little steep."

"What do you have to complain about; you're better than I am."

"Alright, if that's what you want. Five dollars it is."

Mark flipped a quarter into the air as JR declared heads. The quarter landed tails and Mark set his ball on the tee. "Now watch, kid. Maybe learn something from your elders." Mark took a few practice swings, then positioned himself to the ball. The sound of a violent whip preceded a flagellate strike against the ball. The ball took off straight and fast, fading to a small speck in the sky.

It was on the fifth hole when Mark landed in some trouble by the pond. We weren't sure if the ball landed in the water or just at the margin. I kept searching the edge as Mark searched behind me. Suddenly I saw something move in the tall grass. My first instinct warned me of a snake, but as I crept closer, I noticed it was a bird. One of its wings was crippled and it struggled to escape my presence.

"Did you find it?" Mark inquired about his ball.

"There's a bird! I think it's hurting!"

Mark walked over, took notice of the bird.

"Well, you know what we're going to have to do, don't ya?"

"Can we take it home with us?"

"I'm afraid there's no home for this bird anymore. We're going to have to put it out of its misery." Mark waved his club in the air signaling JR who was standing a few yards off the fairway. "HEY JR, WHATA YOU THINK? A 6 IRON?"

Like an ancient sacrifice to the gods, Mark precisely raised the club to the sky. He took a lasting look at me; the skin of his face slowly crimped to sinuous wrinkles. A light reflected off the club face, blinding me just before he swung down to smash the bird's head. Like a newborn butterfly, the bird fluttered away. The wings flapped the neural body closer to the water, away from its now severed head. There were a few more misguided flaps, then nothing.

Mark walked back to the cart as I stood staring at the dead bird, wondering about what happened, feeling guilt and shame pouring through my heart. I picked away at some of the tall grasses and covered the bird's head and body. I felt the need to say something, but I couldn't articulate any words.

"Hey, kid," Mark said. "Don't worry about it." He took a long drink of his beer, then crushed the can in his fist. "It was going to die anyway. Say, you wana drive the cart now?"

A part of me wanted to run. I felt this overwhelming desire to escape. I now desperately wanted to leave everything behind and find a new place far away. No longer was I sheltered, or happy, or safe. I discovered for the first time another side of me, this hidden person caught deep within, someone only strong enough to weep against everything holding him back.

Mark and JR finished the round on the 18th just as the sun was setting. Mark had lost the bet and handed over 35 dollars to JR. We approached the clubhouse and stood next to the concessions. Mark ordered another beer and retrieved his golf bag from the cart.

"Well, whata you think, JR?" Mark said. "Another round at the bar?"

"No, I'm good. Think I'll be heading my way."

"How ya gonna get home? Didn't Maris drop you off?"

"Yeah, but I can walk. It's not that far."

"Hey, we've got room in the car. I'll pull it around."

"No, that's alright..."

Mark quickly grabbed his bag, tapped me on the shoulder, and began speed walking back to the car. I could barely keep up, running almost full speed to his pace. Mark started the ignition and turned the radio up to full volume. The speakers cracked as the song played. We pulled around to the front, darting between incoming cars seeking the valet. We spotted JR and slowed up next to him.

"Hey, man, there's room in the back," Mark yelled out the window.

"No thanks," JR said. "I'll be alright."

"What are you talking about, man? Come on, ride's free."

"You've had too much to drink."

"*What?* Come on. Get in."

"I'll call you later."

JR continued walking. He crossed the parking lot into a field that bordered the golf course. His shadow started to disappear.

"JR!"

Suddenly Mark floored the car into a violent fish tail. The back end of the car swung quickly to the left, as a cloud of smoke rose to the deafening sound of squealing tires. The smell of burnt rubber soon flooded my senses. Fear gripped me. I felt too constricted to breathe. I held tightly onto the arm rest as we sped off down the street.

I looked at Mark out of the corner of my eye and noticed that his face had turned bright red and his lips were pale white. I got the impression that he had forgotten everything—about me, about JR. It was as if I wasn't even sitting in the car with him.

We pulled into the driveway. I immediately noticed that my mother wasn't back yet. As we entered, I noticed a flashing light on the answering machine. Mark walked over and pushed play. The voice was distorted; it crackled, then faded into a synthesized machine voice: *Monday, 6:47 pm. There are no new mes-*

sages. Mark violently ripped the answering machine from the wall and threw it to the ground, shattering it to pieces. I ran to the bathroom, took cover behind the shower curtain. I could hear more things breaking, walls being punched, things being torn. With every form of destruction, the iconoclast's voice howled against a deep repression. After a few minutes, there was silence. Things suddenly changed. I no longer felt the fear. I was now empty and hollow. Numb, yet curious.

I walked out of the bathroom and peered around the corner. There stood Mark, wrapping his bloody hand in a white towel. Throughout the room were broken pictures—some barely clinging to the walls—a tv screen smashed in, a couch ripped by a knife which was now stuck in the chest of mom's Raggedy Ann doll. Scattered along the floor were broken beer bottles, ash trays, vinyl records, torn clothes—every box flipped over and kicked across the room.

Mark noticed me in the hallway, then walked over to the couch and lit up a cigarette.

"Come here," he said. "I'm not going to hurt you. I promise."

I walked over, cautiously stepping around some glass on the floor.

"I'm sorry you had to see this. It's just..." He took a drag from his cigarette. "I'm just not in the right place right now."

Headlights flashed through the curtains. It was mom. She entered the smoke— riddled damage. Her face turned to stone as her eyes widened to the image of a broken home.

"What happened?" she asked in a piercing tone. "Did somebody break in?"

Mark and I remained silent. It wasn't long before she noticed the towel around Mark's hand.

"What happened to your hand? Did you do this?" She approached closer and looked into Mark's eyes. "You're drunk!"

Mark looked up with somber, blood-shot eyes.

"I'm sorry," he softly responded. "It just kinda happened."

"JUST KINDA HAPPENED! JUST KINDA FUCKING HAPPENED! Give me your keys!"

"What? Why?"

"I SAID GIVE ME YOUR KEYS, NOW!"

Mark slowly tried to reach is swollen bloody hand into his pocket, but the pain stopped him from digging too deep. Out of frustration, my mom pushed his arm back and dug into his pocket. She quickly ripped the keys out and grabbed me by the arm. "I'm taking Jamison back to his father's! When I get back I want you gone!"

My mother didn't say a word to me on the way back. The radio remained off and I could only sit and feel the intensity of her thoughts scraping across my skin. She seemed somewhat calm, breathing very systematically through her nose and out her mouth. She maintained a keen focus on the road, driving just under the speed limit, and using blinkers with every cautious merge. I got the sense that she had somehow trained herself to deal with these kinds of situations. For the whole trip home, she never once looked at me.

We pulled into my father's driveway. The engine went silent. My mother took a deep breath, glanced at me, then stared down at her lap. I could see the tears coming. It was if her iron soul was slowly rusting and she had no choice but to feel.

"So... I think it's best that you stay with your dad for a while—at least until I get things straightened out," she said.

"Ok, mom."

She looked at me and smiled. We hugged and I could hear her weep behind my shoulder. She pulled back and wiped the tears from her cheeks. "Ok. Let's go. Your dad is probably asleep. I think I still have a key, so I'm just going to let you in," she said, as she began scouring her purse for the keys.

As I waited outside the front door, I felt the familiar pain inside my stomach. It was like a small knot weaving itself bigger. The pain grew as the knot twisted slowly, almost methodically winding heavier, encompassing more of my stomach. I doubled over begging for relief.

"Are you okay, honey? Come on. Let's get you inside so you can lie down."

The door opened and I saw a silver glint off my mother's eyes. Inside a dim light illuminated the sweat of my father's naked back mounted on Jody, thrusting his hips against her, her legs spread wide. Jody opened her eyes to my father above. Across his shoulder she noticed us and immediately drew his attention off. My father quickly grabbed a blanket and covered himself. Jody sat up and crossed her arms over her breast.

"How did you get in here!" my father exclaimed.

"YOU FUCKING BASTARD!" my mother cried, throwing the keys at his face. She then quickly grabbed me and took me outside. A rush of blood and tears flooded her face. With all her strength she tried to hold on, but it all came out in one big sorrowful burst. *"I'm sorry,"* she said. *"I'm so, so, sorry. I never wanted this for anybody."* I wanted to comfort her, but the pain in my stomach was too much. My legs went numb and I could feel myself fading out. Suddenly the darkness came. Then a light sprinkle of gold dust.

I awoke in my bed. The door was slightly ajar with the hall light on. A shadow moved across the hall and entered my room. Jody stood before me.

"How are you feeling?" she asked in a nurturing tone.

"Fine."

"Well, that's good."

"What happened to mom?"

"Your mom is ok," she said, pulling the covers over my chest. "You were having a bad dream."

"Jody?"

"Yes?"

"Would you ever hurt a bird?"

"A bird? Why of course not. What makes you ask?"

I shrugged my shoulders. I didn't feel like saying anything else.

"So I got you something to help you with your nightmares," she said.

I looked down at the wall. Jumping out of the electric socket was a vivified Batman captured in mid-stride, fist clinched, his cape spread in a bright blue glow. It illuminated my room with a calming radiance against the darkness. A certain tranquility came over me.

"It's a Batman night-light," she said with a peaceful smile. "Now you should get some rest, ok."

She left, closing the door. The whole room instantly turned to a light blue. I looked at the floor and noticed that the gold beads were no longer there. I waited, looked again—but nothing, just the warmth of blue. I prayed for a car, hoping it would bring them back. A few minutes passed and I could hear the faint sound of an engine. I sat up, wide-eyed. Please. The beads. The pool of light. The stars. I wanted them back. Then the car raced past, the tires slashing through wet streets. But only a thin blade of light moved across the window. The sound of the car quickly faded. I pulled the covers over my head and tried to poke holes with my fingers. Maybe I could make my own stars. It won't matter, I thought. Somehow I knew they would never be together again.

☆ ☆ ☆

Alan De Silva currently lives in Morristown, New Jersey.

www.alandesilva.net

For the latest on Boris Jairala please visit Jairala.com

Made in the USA